"Take me to bed, Fletcher," Stevie demanded softly against his mouth.

He wasted no time scooping her into his arms and walking to the four-poster. He set her gently on the bed and reached for her again.

The sensation of skin on skin was sheer bliss. He bent his head and nuzzled her neck, inhaling her sweet scent and committing it to memory. He knew that come morning he had to return to his life. A life that didn't include Stevie Nickerson, even if he wanted it to. She'd made her feelings plain on the topic. He had to take what he was offered and enjoy it. And he did.

He trailed his fingers along her shoulders then down her arms before tracing back up again. She squirmed, her hips pressing against him in silent entreaty.

"Do you like that?" he asked gently.

"So much," she gasped in reply.

* * *

One Night Consequence by Yvonne Lindsay is part of the Clashing Birthrights series.

Dear Reader,

Welcome to book four in my Clashing Birthrights series—*One Night Consequence*!

Stevie Nickerson took back her life after her controlling husband died, and she's vowed never to marry again. She's already lost a child and has no desire to have another. She doesn't count on the turmoil she feels or how she will cope when Fletcher Richmond, her late husband's best buddy from college, reenters her world and she finds herself pregnant with his baby.

Since discovering his father's double life and his and his siblings shock illegitimacy, family and stability has never been as important to Fletcher Richmond as it is right now. But a spur-of-the-moment affair with the owner of the boutique hotel he went to over Christmas, the widow of his best friend, has produced a result, and there's no way his child will grow up illegitimate or without him in their life.

At a crossroads in his life, can Fletcher prove to Stevie that loving him doesn't mean sacrificing her individuality at the same time? Can he really be the man she deserves? Read on and find out!

Best wishes,

Yvonne Lindsay

yvonnelindsay.com

YVONNE LINDSAY

—

ONE NIGHT CONSEQUENCE

HARLEQUIN®
DESIRE™

Recycling programs
for this product may
not exist in your area.

ISBN-13: 978-1-335-73550-8

One Night Consequence

Harlequin Enterprises ULC
22 Adelaide St. West, 41st Floor
Toronto, Ontario M5H 4E3, Canada
www.Harlequin.com

Printed in U.S.A.

Award-winning author **Yvonne Lindsay** is a *USA TODAY* bestselling author of more than forty-five titles with over five million copies sold worldwide. Always having preferred the stories in her head to the real world, Yvonne balances her days crafting the stories of her heart or planting her nose firmly in someone else's book. You can reach Yvonne through her website, yvonnelindsay.com.

Books by Yvonne Lindsay

Harlequin Desire

Clashing Birthrights

Seducing the Lost Heir
Scandalizing the CEO
What Happens at Christmas...
One Night Consequence

Visit her Author Profile page at Harlequin.com,
or yvonnelindsay.com, for more titles.

You can find Yvonne Lindsay on Facebook,
along with other Harlequin Desire authors,
at Facebook.com/harlequindesireauthors!

I dedicate this book to my family,
who have always been my
greatest support and cheer team.

One

Stevie gave the bedspread one final flick before stepping back from the four-poster and observing the room with a deep sense of pride.

She loved the little touches of heirloom Christmas decorations—each one retrieved from boxes in the attic. Everything was finally coming together. Life was good. No, it was fantastic. She was finally achieving her dream of making her family's twelve-bedroom, 140-year-old Queen Anne Victorian home into a successful, luxury bed-and-breakfast boutique hotel.

It had been hard these past eighteen months, but then again, it had been hard for everyone in tourism—heck, in everything, worldwide. But she'd treaded water through it all and now she was ready to start swimming. And as soon as she had confirmation that she could enter into a new loan with the bank, she'd be on her way.

The sound of a high-performance car engine snaking up her driveway warned her of an impending arrival. Strange, she didn't remember booking anyone in, but maybe Elsa had done it before she'd gone on leave. Stevie ran the bed-and-breakfast with two staff—Elsa, who helped with cleaning and led guided hikes in the mountains for their guests, and Penny, whose domain was the kitchen. What the woman couldn't cook or bake hadn't yet been invented.

Stevie turned to the window with a satisfied smile. Yes, everything was coming along according to plan. Her smile faded as she saw the low-slung European two-door coupe glide around the looped driveway and come to halt by the front-entrance stairs. Her lips twisted in disapproval. That car was just the kind of flashy display of wealth her late husband would have raved about. A bitter taste flooded her mouth and she swallowed it back. She hadn't thought about Harrison in weeks, but some things brought him front and center in her mind, and with it, the feelings of inadequacy and sense of dependence he'd fostered in her.

She turned from the window and reset her thinking, reminding herself she wasn't that woman anymore. She was back to being herself, Stevie Nickerson, proud proprietor of Nickerson House. The building had been in her family since the late 1800s several greats grandfather had built the house with timber from the nearby Nickerson Mill and Lumber

Company. These were her roots. This was where she belonged. Where she was happy. And come hell or high water she'd have a happy smile on her face as she greeted their only current guest.

Stevie ran lightly down the main staircase, her hand drifting on the highly polished wooden handrail, decorated with mistletoe and berry garlands, with a sense of familiarity that was second nature. She could navigate this entire place with her eyes closed. It was home. And now she could share it with others. She had reached the reception area when the front door swung open. The sun limned the newcomer, and for the first few seconds, Stevie couldn't see his face. Only the tall, strong outline of his body, the weary set to his shoulders and the well-worn duffle in his hand.

"Welcome to Nickerson House. I hope you had a good journey," she said smoothly as the door swung closed behind him.

And with the door closing, his features became apparent. His hair was swept off his forehead, exposing piercing gray eyes beneath thick dark blond brows, and his cheek bones rose prominently above the stubble on his face and square jaw. Her eyes were drawn inexorably to his mouth. One made up of a chiseled upper lip contrasted by a sensuously full lower one. These were features that were already familiar and embedded somewhere deep inside the darkest recesses of her memories. Features that sent dread pummeling through her and tied her stomach in an uncomfortable knot.

Fletcher Richmond, her late husband's best friend.

Here, in her home. She hadn't seen him since Harrison died. Prior to that, he and Harrison had appeared to have drifted apart and, selfishly, she'd been relieved she didn't have to pretend she was unaffected by his presence on his occasional visits. She'd never stopped to question what had caused the cooling of their friendship, merely putting it down to being on different paths. And, by then, she was starting to feel the cracks in her marriage and they had taken up all of her energy. He'd been among the crush of people at Harrison's funeral and had spoken to her briefly to express his condolences on her loss. Seeing him here, now—it was a shock.

Stevie rested a hand lightly at the base of her throat as if that would ease the tightness that had suddenly constricted her voice, rendering her unable to speak. There had to have been some mistake. She coughed slightly to clear her throat.

"Stephanie?" He looked as stunned as she felt.

"I go by Stevie now."

Before she'd married Harrison, he'd insisted on her using her full name, as it was more befitting the wife of a man aiming for the top. As far as he was concerned, she made the perfect accessory to his political aspirations—provided she forgot her nickname, had her teeth straightened, had elocution lessons and dressed and behaved accordingly. And, stupid, besotted fool that she was, she'd done all that as well as shelved her hotel management degree. All because she'd believed she loved him. Even more stupidly, she'd believed that he loved her.

"Stevie, huh? Why?"

Fletcher didn't waste time coming to the point. He'd always been like that, she remembered. And she also remembered how he was the only man she'd ever met who managed to unnerve her completely with nothing but a glance. Even now, she felt that all-too-familiar rush of blood through her body, the tightening of her nipples in her delicate lace bra and the throb of awareness that pooled in her lower belly. She forced herself to ignore it all, as she always had.

"I've always used it—at least before I met Harrison. Now, I'm sorry. Did you have a res—"

"I had no idea this was your place. Although I do remember Harrison once saying your family was in the hotel trade."

She just bet he had—Harrison had always been the king of spin and had, no doubt, made it sound a lot grander than it really was, too.

Fletcher continued, "I called and spoke with someone yesterday. Booked in for two weeks."

Two weeks? The knot in her gut tightened a notch.

"Let me check," she muttered, stalling for time.

She woke up the computer screen and opened the reservations software. Sure enough, there he was. With a side note from Elsa that he wanted to do some of the local guided hikes. How had she missed this? If she'd have known he was coming she'd have... She'd have what? Canceled his booking? Taken a long trip on a slow boat to anywhere but here? She gave herself a mental shake. This was ridiculous. She was an adult and they needed the business. She hummed a little under her breath—something she'd always done when she was nervous. It had annoyed the hell out of Harrison and she couldn't remember doing it since his funeral. How symbolic it should be Fletcher Richmond who triggered it again.

"Ah yes," she said firmly. "Here you are. You're in the Beaumont Suite. Do you have luggage, Mr. Richmond?"

"Fletcher, please. We're old friends."

Friends? She'd never thought so. He and Harrison had been best buds in college, and in the early days of her marriage, she'd been dutifully paraded out whenever Fletcher was in town. She had never considered him her friend. Especially as the sight of him had always sent an uncomfortable rush of physical awareness through her body. She forced a smile to her face.

"Fletcher, then. So, luggage?"

"Just my pack," he said, lifting said item a few inches and delivering a killer smile in her direction.

He was drop-dead gorgeous any day of the week, but when he smiled, he was seriously dangerous to a woman's equilibrium. But looks, as she knew, were only skin deep. The measure of a man came in how he respected and treated others around him. She shored up her defenses. No doubt he'd be making demands and throwing his weight around within minutes, just like Harrison would have. After all, hadn't her late husband always said he and Fletcher were cut from the same cloth?

"If you'd like to come with me, I'll show you to

your suite," she said stiffly and came around from the protection of the reception desk.

The instant she did so, she felt vulnerable. She wasn't small, but Fletcher topped her by a good five inches and made her feel as if she were less in control. Maybe she ought to start wearing higher heels at work. No, she told herself firmly. She'd promised herself she wouldn't dress specifically to please, or because of a man, ever again. That said, she had her day uniform on, a neat but elegant black dress, short sleeved in summer, long sleeved in winter, paired with low-heeled pumps. Stevie straightened her shoulders and headed to the large staircase that led to the second floor. She could feel Fletcher following behind her.

"Nice place," he commented.

"Thank you. It's been my family's home for five generations."

"Interesting. Harrison never mentioned that."

No, he wouldn't have. Despite the fact her family had always been well-off, they'd never had the stratospheric level of wealth enjoyed by her in-laws. As far as Harrison was concerned, she ought to have been grateful he'd lifted her from her mediocre background and transformed her life. Well, he'd certainly transformed her life, she thought with a twist of her lips.

"Here's your room," Stevie said when they reached the end of the corridor. She stepped forward and opened the double doors leading into what had been the original master and mistress suite and stood back as Fletcher entered. "I'm sure you'll find everything you need here, but if there is anything else, don't hesitate to let me know. Just lift the phone and dial zero."

"Five generations, you say?" Fletcher asked as she started to close the doors and beat a retreat.

She balked a moment, unwilling to share her family history with him, but it was printed in the guest compendium on the table by the window, so she decided on the potted history version.

"Yes, my several greats grandfather built the house for his English bride. There have been Nickersons here ever since."

"It hasn't always been a hotel, right?"

"No. But, after my grandfather died, my grandmother converted it into a hippie-styled wellness retreat, much to the irritation of the locals who thought she was starting a cult. She always used to say that it kept food on the table for her and my dad, so it was worth ruffling a few feathers. The alterations she made at the time, with extra bathrooms and enlarging the kitchen, made it easy to change it into a boutique establishment."

Fletcher chuckled, and the sound made butterflies rise in her tummy. She remembered that about him from before. How his laughter could light up a room and all the people in it. Friends hanging on his every word as he recounted a story, then all sharing the mirth as it reached its conclusion—even her.

"She sounds like a character. Does she still live here?"

"She passed away a couple of years ago. I still miss her. Harrison might have told you that she took me in when I was a baby after my parents died in an avalanche."

"I'm sorry for your loss."

The words could have sounded trite, but oddly from him, they were imbued with a wealth of understanding and compassion.

"Thank you. Now, as I said before, you should find everything you need in your suite. Breakfast can be served here or in the dining room. Just let us know before ten tonight."

"The person I spoke to when I made the booking mentioned guided hikes?"

"Yes, but she is away at present. I can arrange those for you through another provider."

"Or you could take me yourself," he said softly.

"I'm really too bus—"

"I believe it's in the package I purchased for my stay, that I'd be accompanied by someone from Nickerson House on the more demanding trails if so required."

Stevie groaned inwardly but kept her outward composure. "Fine. Then, yes. I could take you myself. If you could give me some notice, it would be appreciated, of course. Now, if there's nothing else?"

She turned to go, only to be arrested by his voice once more.

"Have dinner with me tonight. We can talk about old times."

She closed her eyes a second or two and drew in a calming breath. The only issue with that was that it brought his scent closer to her. A scent of crisp citrus notes with an underlying tone of sandalwood and vital, warm male that she'd all but forgotten. A scent that was as forbidden now as it had been when she'd been married to his best friend.

"Fletcher," she said on a sigh of irritation. "I'm already busy tonight, and to be frank, I would prefer not to rake over old times with you when I've spent most of the past eighteen months trying to forget them."

And with that, she firmly closed the doors between them and walked smartly down the corridor. Her hand shook as she gripped the balustrade. Why had she let him upset her? This was her business, her home. He was a guest here and that was all. He'd be here for only two weeks, and then he'd be gone again. She couldn't wait for that day, but in the meantime, no matter how much she internally railed against the idea, she had to follow the protocols that she herself had set for Nickerson House. His experience here would have to be flawless.

Even if it killed her.

Two

Fletcher stared at the doors wondering what the hell he'd said to so clearly piss Stephanie—no, *Stevie*—off so badly. He'd just wanted to reminisce. Surely that wasn't an unreasonable expectation? She had to be missing Harrison. His had been such a larger-than-life presence. Maybe that's what it was. Maybe the loss was still so raw she didn't want to talk about it. After all, it had only been a little over a year and a half.

He replayed the words Stevie had said before departing. Something about doing her best to forget? A small frown pulled between his brows. That didn't seem right. They'd been devoted to one another, but the woman he'd met today, while still stunning, was not the same woman he'd met as Harrison's fiancée and subsequently, his wife. For a start, there was the name. Stevie. Oddly, it suited her better than the more formal Stephanie. Either way, she obviously hadn't wasted time leaving their marital house and heading back to her childhood home as if she couldn't wait to put that part of her life behind her.

Fletcher expelled a sharp breath and rechecked his thinking. Who was he to tell anyone how to cope with a sudden death in the family? He himself had struggled with the loss of his father almost a year ago. But then again, it was unlikely that Harrison had lived the kind of double life Fletcher's father had, maintaining two separate families—each with two sons and a daughter—and two near-identical businesses, one in Norfolk, Virginia, and another in Seattle, Washington, for thirty-five years. The families only discovered one another's existence when Douglas Richmond had dropped dead in his office in Seattle. Thankfully, the half siblings had bonded in their combined shock and grief and had worked together when there'd been a case of corporate espionage at Richmond Developments in Seattle. But his new family aside, Fletcher still recalled the shock of discovering his dad, a man he'd revered all his life for his integrity and devotion to family, had been a fraud. Unravelling his complicated life was still causing issues.

It was Fletcher's weariness of dealing with those very issues that had seen him take an uncharacteristic leave of absence from Richmond Construction for two weeks in the mountains. Here, he hoped to recharge and unwind. To somehow reset himself after what had been a tumultuous year. The last person he'd expected to see in Asheville was Stephanie Reed.

It wasn't that he hadn't thought about her since Harrison's demise in a fiery plane crash. In all honesty, he'd barely been able to get the memory of her shell-shocked expression at Harrison's funeral out of his mind. Every instinct had urged him to offer her comfort, but he had reminded himself firmly that on every visit to their home, she'd shown that he was someone to be tolerated, not welcomed. He'd wondered briefly if she'd been envious of the friendship he and his buddy had shared. Theirs had been a relationship based on an easygoing rivalry. Each striving to outdo the other, whether it had been with grades in class, achievements on the sports field or the pretty girls they'd had fleeting relationships with. Fletcher had graduated top of their year, with Harrison only a few points behind him, but Harrison had won the greatest prize. He had seen Stephanie first, and married her.

She'd changed so much. Gone were the designer shoes and immaculate clothing, the sleek hair perfectly straightened to fall just to her shoulders—never longer—the perfectly enhanced features and exquisitely shaped brows and the subtle French-manicured nails. Now, despite the tailored dress she'd worn, her hair was a loosely curled tumble over her shoulders. He'd bet that when it was gently pulled straight, it would reach halfway to her waist. His hand had itched to stroke it, to discover if it was as silky soft as it looked. Her skin had been clear and fresh instead of perfectly made up. If anything, she wore only a touch of mascara to highlight those stunningly expressive brown eyes of hers. If he hadn't been mistaken, her fingernails had been painted a bright coral to match her lipstick, rather than the oyster pink she'd always worn in the past. She even spoke differently—the cadence of her slightly husky voice less formal.

It was like she'd reinvented herself completely and he still found her so damned attractive this vacation was going to be a weirdly pleasant kind of torture. Maybe spending time with her would be a bit of light relief during his stay, but then again, he wasn't into forcing a woman to do his bidding. He'd been fortunate all his life that people had generally liked him, which was part of what had made Stephanie— Stevie, he corrected himself again—so appealingly challenging.

Fletcher threw his duffle on the chair and shucked his sneakers before stretching out on the bed. He let his head sink into the thick feather pillow. A faint scent of lavender emanated from the fabric and he breathed it in deeply. He hadn't realized until this moment how tense he'd been on the six-hour drive here. He felt his body ease into the bed with a sense of well-being he hadn't experienced in a very long time.

This was what he'd come here for. To take time to stop and think. To get his thoughts in order. To just be himself for a while.

Ever since he was young, he'd had to take on the role of man of the house half the year when his father was away on "business." Or what he now knew was taking care of his other family.

So Fletcher had to be his mother's support, stand in for his siblings, pick up the slack at the office, answer to the board. All his life, he'd been the fixer for the family. The one who solved the problems and took care of others. And then his life had come to a crashing halt. He couldn't fix his father's betrayal, his mother's lies, his family's grief, his fiancée's demands to stop the scandal. For the past year, he'd done his job but there had been no satisfaction in it. And he realized he was tired.

When was it going to be time for someone to take care of Fletcher? For him to do what he wanted? These two weeks might give him some insight.

It was growing dark outside when he awoke, shocked to realize he'd rested the better part of two hours. He never napped. In fact, these days, he rarely slept well, and yet he felt more refreshed now than he had in ages. And he was starved. He knew Nickerson House didn't offer dinner as part of their accommodation package, so he'd have to leave and find a nearby restaurant. He still felt a sting at Stevie's refusal to join him for a meal, but hopefully, she'd be able to recommend somewhere nearby.

He took a quick shower and changed into fresh clothes. Grabbing his jacket, he headed out. Downstairs, all was quiet. Surprising, really. He'd expected there to be other guests in the large sitting room off the reception area. A log fire burned cheerfully in the wide fireplace, and he spied a tastefully decorated

Christmas tree in the corner that had to be at least ten feet tall. It looked like a perfect spot to unwind with a drink after a day on the trails or snowboarding on the nearby ski slopes, but it was completely empty. Was he the only guest here, or was it too early for others to mingle?

Fletcher shrugged and carried on down the hallway, following the sounds and scents that came from the end of the passage. Whatever was cooking, it smelled divine, and his stomach growled with anticipation. The door at the end of the hallway was slightly ajar, and he heard Stevie in conversation with another woman. He courteously knocked on the door before entering, and both women swung around to see him.

"Is there a problem, Mister—I mean, Fletcher?" Stevie asked. "Is the phone in your room not working?"

"No, no problem and I'm sure the phone is fine. I was just wondering if you could recommend somewhere for dinner?"

The other woman stepped forward, wiping her hands down the front of her apron before holding out a hand. "Hi, I'm Penny. I'm the cook here and we have plenty to share this evening. Since you're our only guest right now, why don't you join Stevie and me? If you're happy to eat casually with us, that is."

Fletcher saw Stevie shoot daggers from her eyes at the cook.

"I'm sure Fletcher would rather head out to a restaurant than eat with us," she said sharply. "Let me get a pen and paper, and I'll list a few places with their addresses for you. Nothing is too far away."

"No, that's okay. I'm happy to eat in. Thank you, Penny," he said with a smile.

For a second, Stevie looked annoyed, then flustered, then downright pissed off.

"Fine," she said, tightly. "I'll set another place."

"I'll do it," said Penny bustling over to a drawer and grabbing a place setting from it before laying it on the scarred wooden table in the middle of the kitchen. "Sit yourself there. Dinner will be ready shortly. Perhaps Stevie could offer you a drink? Maybe a glass of that merlot we opened last night?"

"That sounds perfect," Fletcher said with a grin in Stevie's direction, "if it's not too much bother."

He could see she was battling with the urge to tell him the truth that she was mightily bothered by him being here, but she remained civil.

"Not at all," she said in a voice that was perfectly modulated but absolutely devoid of feeling.

Penny gave Stevie a quick glance as she crossed the large kitchen to a dresser at one end and lifted down a wine glass from the shelf. She poured a generous serving of red wine, then brought the glass and the bottle over to the table before filling the other two glasses that sat at the other place settings.

"Sit," Penny said. "I can serve."

Stevie nodded her head smoothly, but Fletcher caught a glimpse in her brown eyes of a spark of something else. Irritation again, he expected. She clearly didn't want him here. He probably shouldn't have accepted Penny's invitation to stay and eat with them, but everything about Stevie intrigued him. Besides, he had nothing more pressing to do than to try to figure her out.

Penny brought three bowls of salad to the table, then a large, covered dish, which she placed in the center. She added a woven basket of dinner rolls that she'd taken straight from the oven. She lifted the lid from the covered dish, and instantly, Fletcher identified the source of the delicious scent that had enticed him here.

"Oh, Penny," he said appreciatively. "Based on that aroma alone, I think I'm going to have to ask you to marry me!"

"Oh, go on with you. I'm far too old for the likes of you. Stevie would be more your kind of gal, wouldn't she? Besides, my husband might have some objections to me up and marrying some handsome young man from out of town." She laughed heartily and began to dish up the rich beef stew onto plates. "Help yourselves to bread and butter. Don't be shy. There's plenty here."

Fletcher looked across to Stevie. "So, what do you say, Stevie? Should I marry you instead?"

He kept his tone light and teasing but saw instantly that he'd gone too far when her face froze into harsh lines.

"No," she answered succinctly.

"Does that mean you'll think about it?" he pressed, still in a teasing tone.

"No, it means I'll never marry again." She turned

to Penny, who sat opposite Fletcher at the table. "If you'll excuse me, I'll take my dinner through to my office. I have plenty of work to get through this evening."

She rose and grabbed a tray from the cupboard behind her and loaded her dinner and her glass of wine on it and left. Fletcher watched her retreating back, lost for words. As the kitchen door swung closed behind her, he turned to Penny, who looked equally baffled by her boss's sudden departure.

"Was it something I said?" he asked, in all seriousness.

"Looks like you hit a nerve. But that's not your fault. She never talks much about her marriage, but she was a very different girl when she came home from the one who went away to college. Either way, I'm sorry we made you feel uncomfortable. Now, can I dish up some more beef stew for you? Refresh your wine?"

Fletcher said no to both things, and he and Penny spent the rest of the meal discussing Asheville and what he could see and do around town during his stay. Turned out that Penny had worked for the Nickerson family for more than thirty years, and she had a wealth of knowledge about how he could spend his time.

But when he left the kitchen to return to his room, he noticed the light shining around the closed door of what he assumed was Stevie's office, behind the reception desk. Should he go and apologize for upsetting her? He took a step toward the door but halted

himself before he could raise a hand and knock. She'd
made it clear she didn't want his company. He needed
to respect that she'd sought her own space and that
that space was away from him.

Again, he was left wondering what he'd missed
about her and Harrison. When she'd changed her demeanor at the table, she was like the Stephanie Reed
he'd known of old. But having seen the difference in
her, he was left confused. Which one was the real
Stevie? And why did it matter so much to him to
find out?

Three

She heard his measured footsteps on the broad wooden-plank floorboards. Heard him stop. Every cell in her body went tight with anticipation, wondering if he would be the next thing coming through her door. Retreating like that had been childish. The person she had clawed her way back to being was better than that. Could state where she stood on a subject without apology. So why had she run?

Did she not trust herself around him? Was that what it was? He'd always unnerved her, physically and emotionally, in ways she had never dared try to understand. It had been easier to attempt to ignore him. Oh, sure, she'd been polite, but she'd always kept her distance. Now, with him in her home, her business, that was going to be nigh on impossible. Especially with Elsa on leave.

The footsteps began again, this time headed for the main stairs. She heard the third step creak, the way it always had for as long as she could remember. Safe in the knowledge he was returning to his room, she let go of the breath she'd barely realized she was holding. Her dinner still sat, uneaten, beside her on the tray. She'd drunk the wine, though. Maybe she ought to reheat her plate.

In the kitchen, Penny was still bustling about. The older woman turned as Stevie entered. Penny crossed her arms under her ample bosom and stared at Stevie.

"What?" Stevie asked, refusing to make eye contact with the woman who had been her mother's best friend and who knew her probably about as well as anyone else on the planet.

"Are you going to tell me what that was all about?"

"He was Harrison's best buddy from college. They were peas in a pod."

"You think?"

"I know," Stevie said firmly and popped her plate in the microwave and pressed the reheat function.

"Seemed like a better kind of man to me."

"Looks can be deceiving."

"Well, that's true enough. So, are you taking him hiking tomorrow?"

"Tomorrow?"

The internal phone on the wall began to chime, the caller ID showing Fletcher's room.

"That'll be him now," Penny said. "Are you going to answer it?"

Stevie walked woodenly across to the phone and lifted the receiver. "Hello, this is Stevie."

"Hi, I wasn't sure if I could bother you when I came by your office. Are you free to talk?"

Fletcher's voice sounded all too intimate in her ear and sent a frisson of awareness along her spine.

"I have a few minutes," she conceded under Penny's watchful gaze.

"Good. I was hoping you would be free tomorrow for that hike?"

He mentioned the trail, and Stevie almost sagged with relief. It was an easy one and didn't require a guide, so she said as much.

"Of course, we'll drop you at the trailhead if you prefer not to leave your car in the main parking lot there, and we'll provide you with water and a packed lunch as well," she added.

There was a silence at the other end, soon followed by a frustrated sigh.

"Stevie, what do I have to do to get you to spend time with me?" he asked.

She felt Penny's eyes boring into her back. She really needed to turn the receiver volume down on this phone as it was obvious Penny could hear every word said on both ends of the conversation.

"Fletcher, I—"

"Look, I don't know what I've done to offend you, but I would like to put that to rest and clear the air between us. Do you think you could accompany me tomorrow so we can talk this out?"

"Go on. Give the man a break," Penny whispered from across the kitchen.

Stevie knew when she was defeated. "Sure, fine. Breakfast is at eight. We will leave at half past and be on the trail by nine. Good night, Fletcher. I'll see you in the morning."

With that, she hung up the receiver and turned to face Penny.

"There," she said with her hands on her hips. "Are you satisfied?"

"Oh, no," Penny laughed. "Not nearly. But I'm heading home to my man now. He's on day shift this week, so I'll be satisfied soon enough. You should try it sometime."

She laughed again as Stevie colored up.

"Penny, that definitely falls in the TMI zone."

Penny just winked in response. "No shame in being in love. Good night, Stevie. You rest up well. You're going to need your energy tomorrow."

Then, with another wink, Penny let herself out the back door. Stevie remained frozen in place as she listened to Penny's car start up and drive away. She started as the microwave pinged to say it had finished warming her meal, but she realized as she took the plate from the microwave, she'd lost all appetite. Instead, she tipped her food into the scraps bin to feed the chickens they kept for fresh eggs and put her plate and glass in the dishwasher.

Although it was still early, she might as well turn

in, she decided. She'd need to be up at dawn to complete the loan application for the bank, especially as the time she'd set aside to do that tomorrow morning was now being taken up by a certain guest. Stevie shook her head. She was hardly in a position to protest having a guest in her establishment. He was the only one right now, after all. She really needed to boost occupancy rates to make Nickerson House look like a better investment for the bank, but bed-and-breakfast competition was stiff in town. Until she had the funds required to finish off the east wing for her planned luxury accommodation and spa facility, she just had to hope the bank would be prepared to invest in the hotel's future.

She took the back stairs to her suite of rooms on the third floor. Still in the same condition as they'd been since before she went to college, the small living room, bedroom and en suite bathroom were shabby but comfortable. A lot like the rest of the house had been before she began the restoration. She'd been lucky to have excellent craftsmen and women to call on in town. People who were good with their hands and more about preserving the historical integrity of a building than in ripping parts out to replace them with modernity. And to be honest, while she loved the pomp and formality of the guest bedrooms—especially the Beaumont suite, which had been her grandparents' rooms—and the formal reception rooms, like the parlor, the library and the dining room, she loved the quirkiness of some of the older rooms that hadn't yet been updated. She could see her grandmother's touch in every one of them and was looking for ways to incorporate that in the refurbishment somehow, too.

So many plans, she thought to herself as she readied for bed. And with a healthy cash injection she could bring them to fruition so much faster. Her grandmother had always cautioned her as a child to walk before she could run, but Stevie really wanted to sprint ahead with this idea. With accommodation rates slowly climbing around town, she knew she'd be able to create a niche that set her business apart. She desperately wanted to make it work—to prove her worth, to herself if to no one else.

And, maybe, just maybe, having Fletcher Richmond here wasn't such a bad idea. The man had corporate contacts that would be a gold mine for her purposes. She needed to change her attitude and make sure that his stay here was the kind of thing he wanted to tell others about. And, as difficult as that might be, it started with making tomorrow memorable for all the right reasons.

Fletcher was just out of the shower and still drying himself when there was a brief knock at the door to his suite. He swiftly draped the towel around his waist and moved to the door. He was surprised to see Stevie there with a large tray perched on one arm and laden with a pot of what smelled like freshly brewed coffee and a couple of covered dishes.

"Good morning. Breakfast is served," she said breezily. "Where would you like it?"

Before he could answer, she'd swept into the room and was walking toward a small table with two chairs that was set in front of a deep bay window overlooking the property's gardens. She turned and gave him a smile that sent a sudden bolt of heat through his body. And here he was, dressed in nothing but a towel and a few random drips of water. Despite the very efficient central heat, he felt a run of goose bumps raise on his skin.

"You didn't need to go to this bother for me. I was planning to come downstairs for breakfast," he said, ensuring the towel was firmly hitched at his waist and willing his body parts to behave.

"It's all part of the service. You didn't specify any food allergies or specific requirements with your booking, so I hope this will be okay. I'll leave you to enjoy it and see you in half an hour," she said efficiently.

"Yeah, sure, that's fine. Look, Stevie, I feel as though we got off on the wrong foot yesterday. I—"

"Please, say no more. I apologize unreservedly. I was shocked to see you, and I let that color your welcome to Nickerson House which was unkind and unprofessional of me. I assure you that things will be different from now on and for the rest of your stay."

"Stevie, you don't need to apologize."

"Well, it's done now," she said with a small smile. "See you soon?"

"Yes, I'll be ready on time."

"Good. Oh, and leave your tray. Penny will be up

later to collect it and service your room." She gave a nod, then left.

He didn't waste any time. He dragged on a pair of warm socks and cargo pants, together with a merino long-sleeved T-shirt before lacing up his hiking boots. He couldn't remember the last time he'd worn them, and they felt unfamiliar on his feet. Then he poured himself a mug of coffee, doctored it with cream and sugar, and took a long sip of the brew. Lifting the covers from the dishes revealed lightly herbed scrambled eggs with grilled bacon and a generous serving of sourdough toast with real butter. His mouth watered and he immediately began to eat, demolishing the meal in record time.

He ended up in the lobby at twenty-five minutes past eight and was pleasantly surprised to see Stevie already waiting for him with two lightweight day packs at her feet. She gave him another of those smiles as she passed over a pack.

"You have two water bottles and some fruit, protein bars and a cold chicken-and-salad sub."

"That sounds like a lot, especially on top of that breakfast."

"You'll burn it off," she said with a glint in her eye. "The track is relatively uncomplicated but there are some steep sections that will test you if you're out of shape."

He laughed. "Are you suggesting I'm out of shape?"

Fletcher felt her gaze drift over his body as if it were a palpable thing, and his temperature rose another notch. If she could do this to him with a look, what would it be like if she touched him? He swallowed to moisten his suddenly dry mouth.

"I wouldn't say out of shape, but you do look as though you've lost weight since I saw you last," she commented before bending to pick up her pack.

He told himself to avert his gaze from the form-fitting leggings she wore and the way they hugged her butt, but his eyes didn't quite get the message. Even though the black fabric hid everything, he'd never seen her in anything quite so revealing. She straightened and he flicked his gaze to her face. Stevie had secured her hair in a single braid down her back. It made her seem younger somehow, less closed emotionally. She looked at him as if waiting for his response and he had to fight to remember what she'd just said.

"Oh, yeah. Well, it's been a tough year since Dad died. Food was pretty low on the list of priorities."

"You lost your dad? I'm so sorry to hear that. I didn't know."

He grimaced. "You're probably one of the rare few. There was a bit of scandal involved, which made everything that much harder to deal with. But enough of all that, let's get this show on the road."

For a second, she looked as if she wanted to say more, but then she nodded and opened the front door and gestured for him to precede her. As he passed her, he caught a whiff of a light fragrance that reminded him of jasmine and honeysuckle. Sweet and light and innocent. It seemed at odds with the woman he remembered, but then, everything about Stevie Nickerson was at odds with Stephanie Reed. It made him want to peel back the layers and discover the real woman.

At the bottom of the stairs, stood a rough-and-ready 4x4. He glanced at Stevie.

"This is yours?"

"Yup, sure is. Climb in."

Climb was the operative word, he realized as he got into the passenger seat. Somehow, he'd never pictured her driving a vehicle like this. It was all work and no play, that's for sure, and it ran well, he discovered as Stevie drove to the trailhead. She spent the journey pointing out local landmarks and places he might like to visit during his stay, and he made a mental note of some of them. When they got to the parking lot, it was pretty much empty. Stevie rolled the 4x4 to a stop and jumped out, grabbed her pack and slung it onto her back in a smooth movement. Fletcher followed suit.

The air was crisp and cool and the sky blessedly clear, promising a fine morning.

"You'll probably need to lose the jacket as we get going," Stevie commented as she headed to the trail entrance, with him following close behind. "We'll be generating our own heat before too long."

Fletcher stumbled slightly. Generating their own heat? He could think of ways he'd much rather do that with a beautiful woman like her, other than hiking a mountain trail. But she was as off limits now as she had ever been. She'd made that abundantly clear and he respected that. He forced his thoughts away from the metaphorical path they'd begun to lead down and focused instead on the actual path ahead. *Start a conversation*, he thought. *That will help.*

"Stevie?"

"Hmm?" she said from a couple of yards ahead of him.

"Why did you leave Raleigh?"

She stopped in her tracks and turned to face him. Her brown eyes looked troubled. "Why do you want to know?"

"Just curious. If you'll forgive me, and I mean no offense, I feel like the person you are now and the woman I met as Harrison's wife are two different people."

She drew in a breath and closed her eyes briefly, as if she were carefully choosing her words to answer with. Her eyes sprang open again and there was nothing soft or sweet about her expression.

"It's complicated," she said bluntly.

"So, tell me about it," he coaxed, drawing up beside her.

"Look, Fletcher, it's in the past. Does it really matter?"

"I'd like to understand. Help me, please?"

She blew out a short huff that was visible in the chill air around them. "Fine, since you insist. You remember how Harrison always wanted a political career?"

Fletcher nodded.

"Well, that included having the right kind of wife by his side. Someone who was intelligent but malleable and who wouldn't rock the SS *Harrison* on its voyage to the White House."

"Malleable? You don't strike me as someone who would change solely to please another. Again, no offense intended."

She laughed but there was little humor to the sound. "You can be sure I will never be like that again. And, in answer to your question, it was important that his life partner be someone he could mold into the *right* kind of woman. Not only someone his parents approved of but someone he could be proud to have on his arm. You know, how he was about name-dropping with his designer suits. Because I thought I loved him, I made a lot of changes."

This time there was no mistaking the bitterness in her tone.

"Wow, are you sure we're talking about the guy I went to college with? Good Time Harry?"

"You asked. I answered. Now, shall we keep walking?"

She turned and began to stride away, but Fletcher was quick to catch up to her. He stopped her with a hand on her elbow.

"Stevie, hold on a minute. I'm sorry. I had no idea."

"It's not your fault. No one did."

"He…he never hurt you, did he?"

"Like, physically?"

She looked at him in surprise and he nodded.

She shook her head. "No, never physically. And to be honest, expecting me to fit his requirements wasn't exactly cruelty, either. He just didn't want *me* but who he imagined I could be. And I let him change me."

She made it sound so clinical. As if she had been nothing more than clay to be molded. Galatea to Harrison's Pygmalion.

"I thought you were happy together."

She sighed heavily. "I did, too. To be honest, looking back, I was prepared to do anything to make him happy. Anything. But things were already difficult before he died. Once he was gone, I had to reclaim the person I was before. I needed to, for my own sanity. I needed to return to my roots, to where I was happiest in my life. I won't change again, not for anyone. I have finally learned to be true to me."

Fletcher realized he still held her elbow and let his hand drop. The second he did, she continued walking, and he followed behind in silence. The track was well maintained and moderately difficult, so it wasn't too hard to examine his thoughts without doing something stupid like stepping off the trail and getting lost. Was she telling the truth? The way she'd painted it, Harrison had been manipulative. Sure, she'd admitted she let him change her, but if he'd fallen in love with her the way she was, why force her to be someone else? None of it rang true with the man he'd known and admired, but he had to admit that Harrison's career goals had always been political and he had been single-minded with purpose. Was that what had made him treat Stevie that way?

If Fletcher had known about it at the time, he'd have...what? What would he have done to change things? He'd respected his friend enough that he'd shown no personal interest in Stevie from the first day he'd met her, even though his attraction to her had been swift and strong. If he hadn't believed it was a dick move to compete for a friend's girlfriend, he probably would have tried to win her from Harrison. Where would they all be now if he'd tried? He shook his head and muttered under his breath. Here he was, assuming he'd have been able to sway Stevie from the man she'd professed to love. In his own way, he was treating her as if her thoughts and feelings on the matter were subservient to his.

"Did you say something?" Stevie said from slightly up ahead.

"No, just cursing under my breath."

"Do you need to take a break?"

"I'm not struggling, but I wouldn't mind being able to stop and take in some of the scenery."

Her lips twisted in a rueful smile. "I'm sorry. I'm being a terrible guide, aren't I?"

"No, you're doing just fine. In fact, I'd rather I was here with you than anyone else."

Their eyes met and meshed, and he couldn't mistake the shock in her eyes. Shock that was swiftly followed by something else. Something deeper and darker and layered with heat. He took a step closer, his hand outstretched.

Four

"No," she said succinctly. She started to walk again.

He stood there watching for a while, wondering what the hell had just taken place and what he'd thought he was going to say. Or do.

"Stevie, hold on a minute. I'm sorry I've upset you."

"You didn't upset me," she said waiting a good six feet away and with a troubled expression marring her features.

"Well, whatever I did, I apologize. I appreciate you bringing me out here. It really is beautiful."

His view truly was beautiful and he wasn't talking about the stunning vista. She looked amazing. Her cheeks were lightly flushed with exertion, her eyes bright, and the sun shone on her hair, casting a rich nut-brown hue through it. Even with it braided back off her face, his fingers still itched to reach out and touch it. To tease the escaping tendrils and feel their softness.

"It's one of my favorite hikes. Farther on we'll reach the old homestead. We can stop there and explore for a bit if you like. This time of year, the ruins are more exposed. I used to love visiting them when I was a kid. I had a big imagination and could lose myself there for hours, if my grandmother would let me."

"And did she? Let you?"

"Never for as long as I wanted her to," she admitted with a wistful laugh.

"I bet you were a cute kid."

"I was gawky. Frizzy hair, big mouth, clumsy. Took me a few years to grow into myself."

Fletcher had the sneaking suspicion that even with that description he still would have found her fascinating. There was something about Stevie that drew him. It was one of the things that had made him withdraw from his closeness with Harrison once they were married. It wasn't good manners to find yourself yearning for your buddy's wife. Not that Stevie ever gave him any encouragement in that department. Actually, she'd almost been the opposite. Cool, but not unkind. A great hostess, but not exactly welcoming when he was there. It had been perverse of him to insist she accompany him on this hike. While there was a gradient to ascend, it wasn't overly tough nor was it dangerous, and the track was in good shape. He certainly could have done it alone.

But that unreasonable side of him was glad he'd been insistent. He'd felt lonely for too long, and some company, even if reluctant, was better than his own. Lonely? He thought about it for a minute. Alone, was more like it. And while it had never bothered him before—and he'd been quite happy with his own company ever since Tiffany left him after the scandal regarding his father's double life—a gaping hole had begun to open in his world. A hole he couldn't quite define, nor did he know how to fill it. It was part of the reason he'd taken this break away from Norfolk, away from his family and his work commitments. The past year had seen him bear a lot on his shoulders, his mother's anger and resentment toward his dad being the heaviest burden.

The irony, of course, was that it was Eleanor herself who caused a lot of the scandal. Not that Douglas wasn't equally to blame for getting his underage girlfriend pregnant. But it was Eleanor who had gotten her parents' housekeeper to sign off on the parental permission for her marriage to Douglas. Eleanor who had continued the lie that her marriage was the legal one even after learning about his other wife and children.

In recent months, Mathias and Lisa, his brother and sister, had withdrawn from their mom. Eleanor Richmond's bitterness at her deception being discovered had been almost worse than the loss of their father.

They'd all been relieved when she'd announced she was moving to Florida to get away from the embarrassment and scandal. But to Fletcher, she'd always be his mom, and he would always look out for her. Unreasonable blame and demands notwithstanding.

Fletcher drew in a long deep breath and let it go again. He'd promised himself he wouldn't dwell on the past while he was here. This was supposed to be his respite. A respite to figure out what he wanted in life and how he was going to make it happen. He'd been the rock that had anchored his immediate family for the past twelve months, and it was time now to let them all swim on their own. He didn't plan to abandon them altogether, but for a long while he'd put everyone else's cares and worries ahead of himself. It was time to allow himself the opportunity to decide what *he* really wanted in his life. Hell, he was thirty-six and what did have to show for it? He'd always imagined that by now he'd be married, maybe even have a family of his own, yet all he had was work and more work. It was time for change.

"Not much farther to the ruins," Stevie said from a few paces ahead. "How are you doing?"

"I'm all good," he insisted.

"I heard some heavy breathing there. I can slow the pace if you like."

"Nah, just too busy in my head. The pace is fine."

"I know what that feels like. Do you want to talk about it?"

"No. I'll work through it. Being here helps."

They fell silent and continued to walk steadily. When Stevie stopped and gestured around them, Fletcher drew alongside.

"There's a sign over there that gives you a bit of history and shows a map of the layout here. Rattle-snake Lodge itself was built as the summer home for the Ambler family in the early 1900s. Apparently, they hosted some big events here with a lot of guests. Kind of hard to imagine when you look at it now, though, right?"

Fletcher grunted his agreement and walked over to the information board. He wandered around for a long time, picking out where the various buildings had been, or at least as many as he could find based on what ruins remained.

"What happened to the lodge?" he asked when he came back to where Stevie had settled on a pile of stones.

"Mrs. Ambler died in 1918, and her husband never came back here after that. Too many memories, I guess. Kind of romantic in a way, but also terribly sad. He sold the property, but then it burned down in 1926—a lightning strike apparently. It must have been beautiful here in its heyday."

"I can see why you'd have enjoyed being here as a kid. A lot of scope for someone with a big imagi-nation."

They sat in quiet contemplation for a while before Stevie turned and looked at him.

"You're not like how I remember you."

He raised a brow. "How so?"

"Less arrogant, for a start."

"You thought I was arrogant?" He pretended to clutch at his chest with his hands. "Ouch!"

She chuckled and he felt himself warm from the inside out at the sound. It was so unrehearsed and so natural.

"Well, I meant it as a compliment," she said, grinning broadly.

Fletcher felt everything in his body settle and center on the woman sitting next to him.

"Thank you."

Silence stretched between them again for a while. The kind of silence Fletcher wished he could fill with questions, peppering her about why she'd thought him arrogant. Instead, he turned his mind back to how she must have perceived him when she and Harrison first married. Fletcher had been standoffish because he'd found himself so strongly attracted to her. He guessed that could come across as arrogance. But that attraction didn't seem to have abated one bit. He closed his eyes, letting his senses focus solely on the woman next to him. On the sound of her breathing, the warmth of her body next to his, the sweet scent of her hair and her skin.

It was torture, but even so, he couldn't quite bring himself to move away.

Stevie felt conflicted. This was one of her favorite places on earth. Especially this time of year when it was rarely crowded with other hikers. She'd never have dreamed that being here with Fletcher would be such a peaceful experience. Even sitting as close to him as she was now, aware of every line of his body—close, but not touching—was unexpectedly comfortable. It would be the most natural thing in the world to lean into him. Instead, she held herself rigid.

He'd closed his eyes, and for a few surreptitious seconds, she scanned his features, admiring the straight line of his nose, the strength of his brow, the enticing softness of his lower lip. She must have made a sound, because his eyes flicked open and he caught her staring. For a heartbeat, it was like that weird moment they'd shared earlier on the trail. A moment when she'd thought he would kiss her. A moment that had terrified her and enthralled her with equal strength.

She'd put distance between them because it was the only way she could hold on to the threads of her composure. She hadn't wanted to feel this way about him—about anybody. She'd made her decisions and she'd rebuilt herself and her self-esteem with it. Now she was building her business. There was no time for anything else, nor did she expect there to be, either. When she'd returned home, she'd been broken. A completely different woman from the naive, hopeful one who'd left for college and who'd married Harrison, four years her senior, the day after her graduation. That woman had believed in love and happy-ever-afters. And while she accepted that not all men were like her late husband, she didn't trust herself not to lose sight of who she was if she entered another relationship. And even if she did do so at some mythical time in the future, it would be on her terms. Not anyone else's.

"Hungry?" she said abruptly and leaned over to unzip her pack.

"Sure, I could eat."

Fletcher grabbed his pack and took out a water bottle first. He opened it and lifted it to his lips, letting the clear liquid pour from the neck. Stevie felt herself mesmerized by the motion of his throat as he swallowed and forced herself to look away and unwrap her sub.

He was nothing like she'd remembered. Certainly not the brash, competitive know-it-all who was virtually a mirror image of her late husband. The discordance unsettled her. It had been far easier to peg him onto the same board as Harrison and dismiss him, but he didn't fit there anymore. Had she made an error in judgment? Was the man sitting beside her, in fact, a truly decent human being?

Stevie gave herself a solid mental shake. It didn't matter either way. She wasn't in the market for a relationship and certainly not with Fletcher Richmond. He ran his family business and lived more than six hours away. They'd likely never see each other after this visit.

Once they'd eaten and gathered up their trash, they walked a little farther past the ruins before looping around and beginning the return to the trailhead where they'd left the car. Every now and then, Stevie would stop to point out a section of interest, so the journey back took longer than the one up. Fletcher didn't seem to mind. In fact, he appeared to enjoy lingering on the trail and taking in the surroundings.

After they reached the parking lot and got into her vehicle, he turned and looked at her.

"Thank you for taking me today. I knew I needed to start this vacation with some time to clear my head. This was perfect. Would I be able to book you again in a few days? I'd love to do another hike with you. Maybe a full day?"

Stevie's first instinct was to refuse—her business was still struggling to recover its pre-pandemic occupancy numbers and aside from a handful of couples coming over Christmas toward the end of the following week, she really only had her usual admin and cleaning Nickerson House to keep her occupied.

"Let me check my calendar and confirm with you. Are you sure you wouldn't prefer to do a hike with a group? There are specific businesses who can arrange that. I'm happy to make recommendations for you."

Fletcher shook his head firmly. "No, I don't want to spend my time with a bunch of strangers. I'm all peopled out."

She let a small smile play across her lips. "Peopled out?"

He nodded. "Yeah, I know you said you hadn't heard a lot about my dad's death, but it brought a lot of unwelcome attention to my family. My mom, in particular, suffered greatly. I've noticed that I come across people in the most random of places who feel they have some right to pass on their opinion of my father and the rest of our family. It's never good or kind. So, if you don't mind, I'd prefer it was just you and me."

"Wow, losing him really did a number on you all, didn't it?"

"It rocked the very foundation of everything we believed in."

She wanted to probe deeper, but Fletcher didn't appear to be any more forthcoming, so she chose to respect his privacy and put the 4x4 into gear. Once they pulled up, she took Fletcher's day pack, together with her own.

"I can take that inside. I was the one using it," he protested.

"It's okay. I'll take them both to the kitchen and empty them out. Did you put anything in here that you need?"

"No, nothing."

"Great. Well, I'll let you know about my availability for another hike later in the week. Did you want to try something a bit more arduous?"

"Sure, I held up today pretty well, for an office worker who hasn't gotten out much in the past year or so."

She laughed. "Gym fit and hiking fit are two different things."

He smiled in return, and for a moment, she was captivated by how it lightened his face and made his usually cool gray eyes shimmer with warmth. She blinked and turned away, heading to the kitchen.

"Stevie?" he called out, arresting her in her tracks.

She looked over her shoulder. "Hmm?"

"Thanks again for today."

She gave him a brief smile and headed for the

kitchen, where she found Penny taking fresh bread rolls from the oven.

"Those look delicious," Stevie commented as she emptied the day packs and wiped them down before placing them in a storage cupboard. "But that's a lot of bread for the two of us. I hope you're going to take some home."

"That Fletcher looks like a man of big appetites," Penny said as she transferred the rolls to a rack to cool. "I don't imagine there will be a lot left after dinner."

"Dinner?"

"You don't expect the poor man to eat alone while he's here, do you?"

"Well, we are a bed-and-breakfast. Not a full-service hotel."

"Ah, go on with you. We always have plenty to share and I'm making my special broccoli-and-blue-cheese soup as a starter. These fresh rolls will go a treat with that."

"What if he's made plans for dinner already?"

Penny stopped what she was doing and settled her hands on her hips as she faced Stevie across the kitchen.

"Tell me, why the avoidance? First, you abandoned him to my tender care last night and you tried to dodge taking him on the hike today. Now you don't want to share a meal with him? Honestly, your grandmother would be ashamed. You know how she was about including strangers at her table."

Stevie felt unaccustomed heat flush her cheeks.

Penny was right. Her grandmother would have made sure that Fletcher was well cared for, no matter what package he'd booked.

"He might not want to join us."

"Why don't you ask him and find out?" Penny said a little testily.

"Why is it so important to you to include him in our evening meal?"

Penny sighed heavily. "Your grandmother would have been the last person to let you molder here while you lick your wounds."

"I'm not licking my wounds!" Stevie said indignantly.

Penny remained silent and gave her the kind of stare only someone who'd known her from birth could manage without putting her back up.

"Oh, okay, fine. That might have been true when I first got back. But I'm better now. More myself."

Penny nodded. "Yes, you are. But there's still work to do. You weren't made to be alone, Stevie. You and I both know that. Now, before you go and interrupt, I know you have borne a lot of hurt. More than a woman your age should have had to deal with, especially on your own. You've been on your own a long time, even when you were married. And I know that your daughter's death, only a month before Harrison's death, will linger forever. But there comes a time when you must let the world back in. I know. When I had my stillborn babies, I thought my world had ended. But then your mamma and your daddy died, and since your grandmother never was the best with helpless little ones, suddenly my arms and my heart were full again—with you. Imagine if I'd never let myself love you because of my own hurts. I'd be so much poorer for it."

The older woman crossed the room and enveloped Stevie in the kind of hug that spoke volumes of her unstinting love for her. Stevie let herself relax into her, hugging her back. Yes, her words had been hard to hear, but they'd come from a place of deep and abiding care.

"As would I," Stevie answered her in a voice choked with emotion. But as she pulled away, she added, "But that doesn't mean I want to share my evening meals with Fletcher Richmond. He was a friend of Harrison's. They were very alike, and I don't care for the reminders of that time."

Even as she said the words, she knew they were a lie, at least the bit about being alike. Harrison would never have accompanied her on a hike like today's— at least not without incessantly moaning about the lack of facilities, hot coffee, etcetera. Fletcher had merely trudged along, enjoying the view and the information and then settling into their simple lunch with gusto.

She blew out a breath. "Okay, fine. Ask him to join us for dinner. I'll be in my office. Come and get me if you need me."

"Thank you, Stevie."

Stevie merely flapped a hand in Penny's direction and headed out the kitchen, letting the swing door flap behind her as she made her way to her desk. It seemed that no matter what she did, she was bound to be spending more time with Fletcher than she wanted to. She may as well harden up and deal with it, she decided. After all, how bad could it be?

Five

Stevie was immersed in a spreadsheet showing a projection of income for anticipated seasonal occupancy levels at Nickerson House. She compared them to the bookings diary on the computer and groaned. Unless she invested some serious money in advertising, she wouldn't get the occupancy. Without the occupancy, she wouldn't get the income to work on the east wing—with or without an extension on her bank loan. And without occupancy, the bank wouldn't see her as a good risk. She'd have to dream up some special packages and see if she could lure more people up for weekday stays through the winter. Weekends weren't the problem—guest numbers were slowly picking up in that area—but while they were the bread and butter of her establishment, she needed the jam and cream as well.

She was startled by a thud at the door, followed by Penny calling out.

"Stevie, could you help me a minute?"

There was a tone to Penny's voice that sent Stevie flying out of her chair, and the second she got her door open, she could see why the older woman had sounded so off. Her right hand was wrapped in a hand towel that was rapidly changing color as an injury behind the towel continued to bleed profusely.

"I think I need to see a doctor," Penny said with a wobble to her speech that spoke volumes as to the pain and fear she was suffering.

"What happened?" Stevie asked, cautiously unwrapping the towel to expose the deep cut across Penny's palm. She quickly rewrapped the towel and continued to apply pressure to the wound as she guided a rapidly paling Penny to a chair.

"I feel so stupid. I've cut cantaloupe the same way every time for years, but the knife slipped, and this is the result."

"Just stay there and I'll call Cliff. He can meet us at the urgent care center. Keep your hand up, okay? And keep pressure on."

"It hurts, Stevie."

Penny sounded quite frightened. Stevie was, too, to be honest. The wound looked nasty and had to hurt like hell. She made the call to Cliff, who agreed to meet them at the urgent care facility, and grabbed her keys.

"What about Mr. Richmond?" Penny asked plaintively.

"Fletcher? What about him?"

"He'll be expecting his dinner."

"I'm sure he'll understand."

To salve Penny's worries, Stevie called his room. Fletcher answered his phone immediately. The sound of his voice sent a weird thrill through her that she forced herself to ignore.

"Fletcher, I'm sorry. Penny has hurt herself and I'm taking her to the doctor. Looks like she needs stitches. I've no idea when I'll be back, so I'm afraid we'll have to postpone the dinner offer."

"Sure, no problem. Do you need help?"

"No, it's okay. My truck is still out front anyway."

"Let me know when you're back."

"Thanks."

She hung up and guided Penny to the truck. As she pulled up outside the urgent care, she was relieved to see Cliff waiting outside.

"I can take her from here," he said in his no-nonsense, capable way. "Thanks for bringing her down."

As the fire chief in town, he was used to coping with emergencies. Stevie watched as he put an arm around his wife and pulled her to him as they walked through the main doors. Something twinged deep inside her chest as she watched them. They'd been married over forty years and were probably as close now, if not closer, than they'd been the day they'd wed. She'd always admired the deep connection they'd had.

Had wanted it for herself for longer than she could remember.

She gave herself a mental shake. She'd hoped for such a connection with her own husband, but she'd made a grave error when she'd hitched her wagon to his train. Harrison's focus had always been, quite simply, Harrison. He'd been raised the perfect son in the perfect family, and nothing but the perfect wife would do. So, he'd made her so, molding her into the kind of woman he wanted by his side—one with gleaming straight hair, perfect teeth and perfect elocution. Someone who could stand by his side at all times, who could organize seamless dinner parties or hostess fundraising evenings without fear of anything being out of place. Someone who did his bidding without question and with her perfect smile in place at all times. Of course, everything had begun to fall apart badly when, during her pregnancy, their daughter's genetic syndrome had been diagnosed. His mother had even had the gall to suggest it had to have come from Stevie's side of the family because, after all, wasn't theirs perfect? They'd encouraged her to remain in the background, not wanting the pregnancy to be in the forefront of people's minds when they saw Harrison.

When little Chloe had died in Stevie's arms only four short weeks after her birth, Harrison had virtually dusted off his hands in relief and had carried on as if his daughter hadn't even existed. Stevie had been left reeling and, deep down, wildly angry with her husband, who'd disregarded their child's existence.

A month later, when the plane he'd been piloting had crashed in mountainous terrain, killing him and his executive assistant, she had been left numb. During the eulogy, Chloe had barely rated a mention. To hear the Reed family's handpicked orator at the funeral, the death of their daughter had been glossed over as little more than a loss Harrison had borne bravely and stoically. It couldn't have been further from the truth. He'd barely acknowledged his daughter's existence.

Harrison's will had been a shock, as had the discovery that the home she'd so lovingly created in the house they'd chosen together, belonged to his parents' trust. Financially, she would receive only half of what she and Harrison had accumulated in their marriage, the other half being held for their children and, in the instance that there were no living children at his death, that portion would go to his parents. Harrison's family had made it clear they would not support her either emotionally or financially, and once she'd picked up the shattered pieces of herself, Stevie knew the only place she could rebuild would be in Asheville, where she'd started from. With people like Penny and Cliff supporting her.

Deciding to remain single had been no hardship, but after watching Cliff's care of Penny just now, it left Stevie wondering who would be there for her if she needed help? She gave herself a stern talking-to on the drive home. There wouldn't be anyone there for her because she wouldn't need anyone, she told herself. She hadn't spent the past eighteen months getting her life back in order only to lose herself in a new relationship. Not everyone was as lucky as Penny and Cliff to find their soul mates.

She parked her truck in the big old garage out back of the house and walked to the rear entrance. The lights were all still on in the kitchen and she shuddered at the thought of having to clean up the mess that would no doubt be there from when Penny cut herself. Stevie let herself in through the back door and was met with a blend of delicious aromas.

"How's the patient?" Fletcher asked from over by the stove where he stirred something inside a big pot.

Stevie looked around the kitchen. No sign of blood or half-chopped cantaloupe anywhere.

"I left her with her husband. There was nothing else I could do, and she didn't need me waiting with them. Cliff will call later and let me know how she's doing."

"And you? Are you okay? You sounded a bit rattled when you called me."

Stevie nodded. She had been rattled. "I'm fine. Just worried for Penny's sake, I guess. But what are you doing in here? I thought you'd be in town, getting yourself something to eat."

"I am getting something to eat. I figured Penny would have already done a lot of the prep for dinner, and I also figured that there might be a bit of cleaning required. And I realized it would be the last thing you needed to worry about if you got back late. I was just going to finish the cooking and then set things aside for you. So you're home just in time."

"Thank you," Stevie said simply. But the words

were nothing compared to the relief and the confusion that flooded her at his explanation. Then reality hit. "You're a guest here. You shouldn't be doing this."

"What?" he said with a grin that sent a pulse of longing through her. "Are you afraid I'll ask for a discount?"

She forced herself to laugh. "That wasn't what I meant at all."

"Hey, it's no big deal. I'm happy to help out a friend."

But he wasn't her friend, was he?

"Can I take over?" she asked.

"How about you set the table for us? And find the soup bowls. Penny made broccoli-and-blue-cheese soup, and it's been making my taste buds work overtime since I stepped in here."

By the time they sat down to dinner together, Stevie felt as though she'd stepped through Alice's looking glass, because everything was topsy-turvy. Fletcher had poured their wine, served their dinner, and now he was clearing the table while she was on strict instructions to stay put in her seat and relax.

"You seem to know your way around a kitchen," she commented, taking another sip of the second glass of wine he'd poured for her.

He shrugged. "I've been living on my own awhile. Figuring out how to use my appliances was a lesson in survival. Turns out I have a knack for it, and surprisingly enough, I enjoy it. It's a form of active relaxing for me. Totally separate from my workday or family stresses. I just focus on what I'm doing and get to enjoy the outcome at the same time."

"Weren't you living with someone else before?"

"Briefly."

His response was so short she didn't feel as though she could press him for more details—nor should she want to, she reminded herself firmly. His life was not her concern. She decided to change the tack of the conversation, bearing in mind what she'd been working on in her office before Penny's injury had called her away.

"Fletcher, would you mind answering a few questions for me?"

"Is there a catch?" he said with another of those quick grins that made her tummy do a weird little flip every time she saw one.

"No, no catch. Just thinking of some market research I was doing before Penny got hurt. With all the available accommodations in this area, not to mention the resorts, what made you choose Nickerson House for your stay? We're farther from town than anyone else."

"I didn't want crowds, and the number of rooms you have on your website showed that even if you were full, I wouldn't be tripping over people."

"Not a fan of crowds?"

"Not anymore. Like I said, a lot of people like to share their opinion on my family and my father's choices. I'd prefer not to hear them."

She nodded slowly. "So, the fact we are boutique style appealed, right?"

He agreed. "That and not being too far to drive to the ski slopes for snowboarding. Why do you ask?"

"Well, as you can see, I'm hardly overrun by people clamoring to stay here. I'm thinking of creating a new marketing campaign, but I need a better understanding of the clientele who'd most likely take me up on special offers."

"You know, you could expand to include meals in the main dining room or maybe even cooking classes when Penny's back at work, this kitchen would really lend itself to that."

She grabbed her phone and began making notes on the screen. "That's a good idea, although I was hoping to go more upmarket eventually with spa retreats. Maybe target the corporate sector and get some business clients who could use a stay here as a bonus for staff or for brainstorming thinktank sessions away from the distractions of the office."

"That's a good idea, too," Fletcher agreed as he sat at the table and lifted his wine glass. "I'm pretty sure Richmond Construction would be on board with that, but I'd need to discuss it with the team."

"Oh, you don't have to—"

"Just think of it as a friend helping a friend," he said. "Besides, you're not quite at that stage yet, are you?"

There he was again, with the friend comment. Maybe she needed to nip that in the bud now.

"Fletcher, we're not friends. Nor were we ever friends."

He looked at her steadily over the table. "I'd really like to think we could be friends. We have a lot in common."

"Please. What on earth do we have in common?"

"Well, we like hiking," he said hopefully. "You agreed to take me on another trail this week, right?"

"That does not a friendship make," she said on a huff of frustration.

"We could discuss your spa plans in more detail. Maybe there's more business Richmond Construction could send your way."

She shook her head. She would not be beholden to anyone, especially this man. "No." Then, realizing how blunt that must have sounded, she softened her tone as she continued. "Look, I appreciate that you're trying to help, but you need to understand that I have to do this on my own."

He raised an eyebrow. "You'd turn away business?"

"Not once I have everything up and running. But I need to be able to prove to myself that I can do this. It was my dream from when I left for college. Yes, getting married derailed that, but I'm back on track now. Finishing what I started. In my own time. On my own terms."

"I can respect that," he said gently and took another sip of wine. "In fact, in some ways, I envy you. It's nice to build your business the way you want to making the most of your family home and tradition."

"Envy me?" she asked incredulously. "You run one of the largest construction companies on the Eastern Seaboard, and you envy me?"

"Yeah, in some ways. It must be cool to be in charge. You can become a success your own way."

She shifted in her chair and looked at him. She'd briefly caught glimpses of unhappiness on his face when he'd thought no one was looking, and she'd put them down to his bereavement and the stress he'd been under. But maybe he was unhappy with more than that.

"It can be daunting," she admitted. "But I'm determined to make a success of it. To put my personal stamp on something. By the way, I do like your idea of cooking classes. When Penny is able, I'll discuss it with her further to see how we could work it out."

Her phone rang. She spotted Cliff's name on the caller ID.

"Excuse me. I need to take this," she said, lifting her phone to her ear.

Cliff rapidly filled her in on the situation with Penny's hand. Stevie ended the call a few minutes later and sighed.

"Not great news, I take it," Fletcher said.

"Not great but not the worst, either. She won't need surgery, but she'll be off for several days, maybe as much as two weeks, and will likely need physical therapy. I'm hugely relieved, for her sake, that it's not as bad as it looked and I certainly don't begrudge her the healing time, but it's hugely inconvenient given that Elsa is on leave at present."

"What can I do to help?"

Stevie shook her head. "No more helping. You're a guest here."

"I am, but I can make my own bed and change my own towels." He shrugged as if those things mattered little to him. "And I can reheat a mean can of soup when required."

She laughed, which she suspected was exactly what he was aiming for. "Don't worry. I don't think we'll be reduced to reheating soup. I have a list of temp staff. It might take some juggling, considering Christmas is next weekend and people will have plans. But I'll manage."

And she would. She was determined on that score. One way or another, even if she had to claw her way through this latest setback, she would get there.

"Look, why don't I clear up tonight and you make some calls? You won't relax until you've got things covered."

"No, it's okay. You go up. You've done more than your share today and I do appreciate it."

Fletcher reached across the table and took her hand. The sensation of his warm, strong fingers clasping hers sent a bolt of awareness through her body. Instinct told her to tug her hand free, but a perverse sense of something entirely female and illogically desperate for reassurance made her stay exactly where she was. Her eyes flicked up to his face and her gaze clashed with his.

"I will do the cleaning up," he said firmly. "And, until you have someone else to assist you, I am more than happy to fill in if it eases your load. Sometimes, Stevie, it's okay to accept help."

She fought to find the words to tell him he didn't

know what he was talking about, but she had the impression that his words came from a place of experience and not necessarily a pleasant one.

"Fine," she said. "But only for tonight. I'm sure I'll have someone by morning. And you won't be doing your own towels and bed linens, either."

She softened her words with a smile.

"If it upsets you so much, then, by all means, make my bed." He winked as he let go her hand and stood to clear the table. For some reason, Stevie couldn't bring herself to move just yet. Instead, she was beset with a visual image of him in the massive and masculine four-poster that dominated the bedroom of his suite. Of his strong body, naked and tangled in her high-thread-count sheets.

Of her there, right alongside him.

No!

She slammed the door on her thoughts and pushed her chair back so hard as she stood that it toppled and hit the tile floor with an enormous clatter. Fletcher spun around from the counter, a look of concern on his face.

"Are you okay?" he asked, concern clear in his eyes.

All she could do was nod. There was no way she could speak. Her throat was thick with unexpected longing, her emotions in a turmoil she couldn't understand. She righted the chair and hastened from the kitchen to her office, humming quietly all the way. She closed the door behind her and leaned against the solid wooden surface as if it were the only thing capable of holding her up. Truth to tell, it probably was right now.

Tremors shook her body. What the heck was going on? She'd made her choices. She wasn't interested in forming a relationship with another person that involved physical intimacy—least of all, Fletcher Richmond. So why was she struggling not to return to the kitchen and grab him to plant the kind of kiss on his lips from which there would be no turning back?

Six

Over the next week, Stevie found a new balance. Keeping clear of Fletcher was her main objective. Thankfully, due to the wonderful community spirit of the town, she had no difficulty getting in a new cook to cover Penny's duties. She found another person who was an experienced guide to take hikes and who wasn't averse to helping her clean. In fact, she'd arranged two hikes for the new guide and Fletcher, so staying out of his periphery hadn't been too difficult. Booking numbers had unexpectedly spiked upward, too, with all her rooms at full occupancy through the Christmas and New Year's period.

The bookings had surprised her, but she wasn't about to look a gift horse in the mouth, and the additional revenue helped with paying her fill-in staff.

She was hard at work in her office, recalculating her budgets for the umpteenth time for her proposal to the bank, when a sharp knock at her office door made her sit up in surprise.

"Come in," she said.

Fletcher wasted no time entering, his presence filling the room and making her wish she'd remained silent so he wouldn't bother her.

"Problem?" she asked.

She stayed seated at her desk, not the best of moves, she realized, as he placed his hands on the wooden surface and leaned forward toward her.

"Exactly why are you avoiding me?" he asked, irritation like a burr in his deep voice.

"I'm not avoiding you," she lied with her fingers crossed in her lap. "Besides, now I have a proper guide to offer you, your hiking experience will be all the more satisfying."

"I prefer being satisfied by you," he said softly.

The words hung between them, loaded with innuendo. She forced herself to remain calm, to keep breathing evenly as if what he'd just said hadn't made every cell in her body leap to full alert.

"I'm sure you understand. I have had a great deal of work to attend to."

"You do realize it's Christmas Day, don't you? Not even you should be stuck in your office doing whatever it is that you've been doing here."

"Hazards of being a business owner," she tried to say breezily. The truth was, since Chloe's death, she didn't feel like celebrating anything anymore. "I'm sure you'd understand that."

"I understand that all work makes Jack, or in your case, Jill, a very dull host."

She colored and leaped to the defensive. "I'm quite sure your experience here at Nickerson House has been everything we promised on our website. If you have a complaint—"

"I know, I'll bring it to the management. Which is exactly what I'm doing. Come on. Join the rest of us for dinner—nice idea by the way. Making it a special occasion for guests who didn't already have plans. Besides, you need the break and you certainly look like you could do with a drink."

"Oh, I couldn't. Not dressed like this," she protested.

"Then, I'll give you half an hour to go to your room and get ready. No more excuses, Stevie. If you're not back in thirty minutes, I'll come and get you myself."

His words were stern, but the expression on his face was anything but. He almost looked as if he were hoping she'd challenge his time limit and make him come and get her. Well, she wouldn't give him that satisfaction.

"Fine, since you asked so nicely," she said acerbically, "I'll get ready for dinner."

"Thank you," he answered and straightened, no longer crowding her space.

But even though he wasn't looming over her anymore, she couldn't ignore his presence in her small office. He was the kind of man who commanded a room, no matter the size, and here, right now, he dominated everything, including her unruly thoughts.

"If you'd let me out?" Stevie said pointedly.

"Sure. I'll see you in thirty minutes. In the dining room."

He grinned as if he'd just won some major victory, and Stevie began to wonder exactly what he was up to. She consoled herself she'd find out soon enough as she powered off her computer and exited her office. As she passed through the space where he'd been standing, she caught a faint whiff of his scent. Her body again did that full-on awareness that she'd started to become accustomed to when he was around. Just a simple primal reaction to an attractive male, she told herself as she trudged upstairs. *Nothing simple about it*, another voice inside her head told her. And her increasingly complicated feelings about him wouldn't be ignored for much longer.

Fletcher watched her go upstairs and felt a zing of excitement. He hoped she'd like the surprise. He knew she'd been avoiding him and he'd been happy to leave it be. She'd made her feelings very clear on the matter and he was prepared to respect that, up to a point.

But no one needed to be glued to a spreadsheet on Christmas Day. He'd caught a glimpse of the schedule on her screen and identified it as a budget projection. He understood them inside and out, but that didn't mean they didn't make his head ache. He preferred to leave their creation to his analyst team. They earned darn good money to deal with those forms.

As long as he had what information he needed, when he needed it, and could report it to the board of directors in satisfactory fashion, then he was happy. But Stevie had no such luxury. Everything about this place began and ended with her. He admired her for her tenacity, among other more physical attributes, but he didn't envy her.

He'd spent some time these past couple of days talking with the temporary staff and a few others in town who knew Stevie well. They all said how much she'd changed when she'd married, but how nice it was to see her back again—and her old self to boot, despite her losses. He'd assumed by that they meant the loss of her daughter, who he'd been surprised to learn about at Harrison's funeral, swiftly followed by Harrison's sudden death and her leaving Raleigh and the life she'd had there. He'd had to admit he'd taken what she'd said about her relationship with Harrison with a liberal pinch of salt. After all, people saw things differently all the time. But what he'd heard about her recently made him even more curious about the real Stevie Nickerson.

He shouldn't be so interested, he kept telling himself, but in all honestly, what was there to hold him back? Aside from her obvious reluctance, that was. And he had to respect that. But what if her reluctance was fear of her own feelings? Wouldn't they be doing themselves a terrible disservice if they didn't at least question the attraction that simmered between them?

He hadn't thought he was open to starting a new relationship. Especially not with all he'd had to deal with in the past year and Tiffany's reaction to the furor over his father's death. He wanted everything on an even keel before he even considered introducing another person into his new life. Hell, if he was telling the truth, he didn't know what he wanted anymore.

Except for one thing. Or to be more precise, one person. Stevie Nickerson.

He wondered what kind of hold Harrison had had on Stevie to have changed her so much from the girl everyone had so fondly talked about here. Was that what she thought love was? Changing yourself to satisfy another? What happened to learning the different, exciting, and even less exciting, facets of another person? Loving them with all their flaws and imperfections. Loving them because of who you became when you were with them and how they made you feel.

Fletcher found himself questioning his own perception of his old friend, wondering if he'd had the wool pulled over his eyes as to exactly what Harrison was like deep down. He examined his memories and could see nothing there. Sure, Harrison had been competitive. But so had Fletcher. And Fletcher had never envied his friend until the day Harrison had introduced him to Stevie—or Stephanie, as she was then. Harrison, had met her while she was in her last year of college and working a part time job at a local hotel where he was attending a fundraiser for the governor. A few months later, they were engaged. Fletcher had flown into Raleigh for the party and was instantly smitten when he was introduced to the new woman in Harrison's life. But there had always been an unspoken rule between the men. You did not poach girlfriends and you certainly did not harbor feelings for the other's fiancée. It hadn't stopped Fletcher being drawn to her, though, or thinking about her often in the intervening years.

That this was her home and the center of her being was abundantly clear in everything she did around the place. Her idea of turning the property into a boutique hotel had been an excellent one. It had fitted in well with what was on offer in Asheville already. And her dream of creating a spa experience for small corporate groups would serve the community well, too. But her stubborn independence might just be her downfall. He'd seen many a dream die before fruition because people wouldn't accept help. He didn't want to see her go through that, and more than anything, he wanted to ensure that she reached her goals however he could. Getting her to accept that help would be the issue.

A sound from the top of the stairs attracted his attention and he looked up, delighted to see her again. She was wearing a red dress that skimmed her body and floated to midcalf, together with a pair of high-heeled black pumps that accented the jet bead necklace she wore around her neck. She'd styled her hair long and loose, in a profusion of unstructured curls. His fingers twitched slightly as he imagined running his fingers through it. Their eyes met and he felt a deep and powerful swell of recognition—as if she were his woman and had been for all time. And then the connection was gone as she averted her gaze and began, with one elegant hand trailing lightly on the polished wooden handrail, to descend the stairs. The sense of recognition built as she drew nearer, making him feel as though they'd acted out this very scene a hundred times before. In his dreams, maybe?

"Have I got something on my face?" she asked as she drew level with him.

"No, you look perfect."

She looked somewhat abashed for a moment. One hand fluttering up to her hair as if she needed to smooth it straight, but then she drew in a breath and let her hand drop beside her once more.

"That's good then, because perfect is exactly what I was aiming for," she said with a flippancy he suspected she was far from feeling.

He smiled and offered her his arm. "Shall we?"

"Why do I have a feeling that I am going to be surprised by what you have in store?"

He shook his head. "Not me. I've not been permitted to do anything. Nor the other guests, either, you'll be pleased to know. I was merely sent to ensure your attendance."

They continued toward the main dining room. As they drew nearer, they were enveloped with sound. Christmas carols played in the background; there was the occasional clink of glassware, and underneath it all, a hum of conversation that sounded warm and inviting. As they entered the room, Fletcher heard Stevie draw in a sharp breath as she took in the decorations and the collection of people there—both guests and old friends of her grandmother's. And, it was heartening to see her obvious delight, when she spied Penny and Cliff, who were seated by the massive fireplace.

"This is just like how it used to be in my grandmother's day," Stevie said in awe. "Whose idea was this?"

"Penny organized it and your stand-in team carried it out. They've done a good job, don't you think?"

"It's incredible."

She was whisked away from him by another person and then another, and by the time everyone was invited to sit at the massive dining table, the atmosphere in the room was lively. Fletcher contented himself with watching her from the opposite side of the table. Extra staff had been brought in to serve and clear, and every time Stevie went to rise from her seat to get something, another person would gently put a hand on her shoulder and encourage her to settle back down.

He thought about his earlier call to his family. They were all at a loss without their father. But they were making their way through it in their own ways. Eleanor with a Christmas dinner together with her new cronies in Florida, Mathias and Lisa with old friends.

The evening drew on, and many of the guests went up to their rooms or went home as it grew late. By the time Stevie had seen Penny and Cliff off and inspected the kitchen, only to realize there was literally nothing left to do, Fletcher stepped forward to take her hand and lead her to the library, where a cozy fire burned on the hearth. He encouraged her to sit in one of the leather wingback chairs at the side of the fireplace and handed her the brandy he'd poured when she'd been fussing in the kitchen.

"Here, I thought you might enjoy this."

She took it and shot him a grateful glance. "Thank you. This is the perfect cap to an unexpectedly perfect evening. What a way to spend Christmas."

"It certainly beats working on budgets and spread-sheets," he commented as he lifted a snifter and inhaled the scent of the very good brandy he'd poured.

"I can't believe I lost track of days like that."

"You've been busy."

Busy avoiding him.

But she'd been in her element tonight. The perfect hostess and clearly admired and respected by all who'd attended. Even the new guests who'd signed into Nickerson House yesterday, still looking a little wan at their first Christmas without immediate family, had loosened up and mingled well with the other guests.

"You've created a wonderful atmosphere here at Nickerson House," Fletcher continued. "I'm sure that your guests will be making recommendations to all their friends and family."

"Let's hope so," she said with a small smile.

"I bet this place has seen a lot of different family Christmases over the years."

"Yes, there are albums up in the attic which record a lot of family gatherings. I was hoping to get some of the photos reproduced and blown up to feature them in a gallery in the east wing. But like a lot of things, it'll need to wait until I have all my ducks in a row." She took a sip of her brandy. "Tell me, what were Christmases like for your family?"

The question took him aback for a moment. Up until last year, he'd never really stopped to think about it too much.

"I guess they were like most family celebrations, except our dad was only there on alternate Christmases and New Year's celebrations. We never dreamed it was because he had a second family. We always just accepted it was about work and he was a very hard worker. He died just before Christmas last year, and to be honest, I don't think the holiday will ever feel the same to any of us again."

"I can't begin to imagine what that must have been like, finding out he had another family."

Fletcher stared into the fire for a while. "It was hell. It made me question everything about my life and what I thought my goals were. It's still making me question them."

"How so?"

"I guess all I ever thought I wanted to do was follow in his footsteps. Be the successful businessman he was. To continue building the corporate empire for future generations." He snorted. "You know, all the clichés you can probably think of. But now I'm not entirely sure if that's where I see myself in another five or ten years. All I know for certain is I don't want to be anything like him. His deception caused us all a lot of pain. I don't know how he ever thought it would end."

"I guess he was counting on not being found out."

"Well, he sure as heck messed that up."

"I'm sorry you were so badly hurt."

He'd heard the words from so many people and from some, yes, they'd been genuine. But from most, there'd been an element of voyeurism thrown in. A curiosity about how a man could maintain two households, families and businesses on two coasts for over thirty years without suspicion. Stevie's tone led him to believe her sympathy was genuine. It was another thing he admired about her. She didn't throw up smokescreens. She said it how it was.

"Thank you." He tipped the last of his brandy down his throat and stood. "It's late. We should probably go to bed."

He saw Stevie's reaction instantly in the way her nostrils flared, her cheekbones colored and her pupils dilated. His words had been simple, not meant to have been steeped in innuendo. And yet his body obviously thought otherwise. Heat flooded through him, especially one particular part of him, and he felt as though he was poised on a precipice, just waiting to leap. Silence stretched between them, and he saw her swallow and moisten her lips, felt his body harden in response.

She put her glass on the small side table next to her with a sharp click, the sound seemingly shocking her out of the odd spell that had enveloped them both.

"You're right. Time to turn in," she said abruptly, and she rose to her feet.

There was barely two feet separating them. All Fletcher needed to do was reach out and he'd be holding her in his arms, pulling her against him. Feeling her softer curves settle against his. Feeling her warm breath on his throat, his lips. She looked up at him again and he knew she felt it—this compulsion that simmered between them. He clenched his hands tight in an attempt to assuage the near overwhelming urge he felt to touch her. And then she sidestepped and moved away.

"Good night, Fletcher. I trust you'll sleep well."

He sure as hell wouldn't. All he could do was watch her back as she walked out of the library and headed for the main stairs, her hair swaying gently with each step. The fabric of her dress caressing the curve of her hips and buttocks as she moved. She'd wanted him, he was convinced of it. But she was far stronger than he. She'd resisted the craving that had been like a third person in the room with them.

But for how much longer? he wondered as he traveled up the now-empty stairs and went to his suite.

Seven

Stevie threw herself even more diligently into work that week. Today, she was focusing on the yard, clearing away debris and trimming back dead wood on a few of her bushes that were already struggling with the onset of winter. Penny had returned to work today with a full medical clearance, much to Stevie's relief. And, even though they'd spoken on the phone daily, she'd missed the older woman's presence. Only one more day until New Year's Eve, and then Fletcher would be leaving. She was almost counting the hours. After spending that time with him after Christmas dinner, she'd become even more conflicted than ever. He was so...so... She dropped her rake, threw her hands up in the air and growled at the air space around her.

"What's up with you?" Penny asked as she came out of the greenhouse with a handful of freshly chopped herbs for tonight's dinner.

"Nothing," Stevie was quick to respond as she picked up the rake and began scraping away under shrubs again.

"Thinking about that nice Mr. Richmond?" Penny asked with a look of innocence in her eyes that Stevie knew was merely a smoke screen.

She also knew that *nice* was definitely not the word she was looking for. *Infuriating*, maybe. Or even *frustrating*. No, it was more than that. She reached into the recesses of her mind. Yes, that was it. *Exasperating*. Fletcher Richmond was one exasperating piece of man flesh. Oh, hell, there she went. Thinking about his body again. She stretched deeper under the shrubs to pull out a particularly hard-to-reach pile of leaves and twigs.

"Not at all. Just having my usual gardening tantrums."

"Sure you are," Penny said with a smirk playing around her lips.

"How's your hand bearing up being back in the kitchen?" Stevie asked, determinedly changing the subject.

"Better than I hoped. I start therapy next week, too. So I'll be back as good as new in no time."

"That's great."

"Been missing me, have you?"

"I haven't missed your cheek," Stevie said with a quick grin. "But to be honest, the house doesn't feel the same without you there, too."

"So, about this Mr. Richmond...?" Penny started with that same faux innocence in her expression. "When are you going to jump him? You're running out of time, you know."

Stevie nearly dropped the rake again. "I beg your pardon?"

"You know. Do the wild thing."

"Penny!"

"I'm not blind, you know. Anyone can see the sparks flying between the two of you. I know you're doing your best to keep out of his reach, but have you considered maybe just giving in?"

Stevie was tempted to ask Penny "Give in to what?" But realized that she would no doubt hear—with great detail—what "what" might be.

"No, I haven't. You know I'm not interested in starting anything with anyone."

"I know you say that, but don't you think that's a crying shame? That gorgeous man, going to waste."

Irritation flared and made Stevie's next words sound snippy. "Well, if you think he's so hot, why don't you have him yourself?"

As she anticipated, Penny hooted with laughter. "Oh, honey. You have it bad, don't you? Take my advice. Act on it before it's too late."

"I won't be acting on anything," Stevie insisted as she switched the rake for a shovel and began filling the wheelbarrow next to her with the pile of garden rubbish.

Penny grunted.

"What?" Stevie demanded.

"Have you asked yourself if you'll regret it if you don't?"

"I beg your pardon?"

"I always do that when I see something I think I really want. I ask myself if I'll regret not buying it or doing it. If the answer is no, then it's simple. I walk away. But if the answer is yes—"

"Is that how you and Cliff hooked up?"

A broad smile split Penny's face. "Yeah, something like that. And it was the best decision I ever made. Take a leaf from my book, my girl. You go work some of that energy off with someone who'll appreciate it instead of in this unforgiving garden."

Stevie watched as the older woman turned and went inside the kitchen door. Penny didn't know what she was talking about. Obviously. She had only the barest idea of how Stevie had lost sight of herself during her marriage—not just herself and the fun-loving girl she used to be, but of everything she'd ever dreamed of, too. No matter how tempted, she would not be acting on Penny's advice. She didn't trust herself not to fall down that rabbit hole again. Not after all her hard-earned gains in learning to live without striving to meet everyone else's expectations.

This was her life, and she was living it as she wanted to. And that was how she planned on keeping things.

A few of the smaller hoteliers in the area took it in turns to host a New Year's Eve shindig for guests. Including arranging shuttles so everyone who wanted to could attend. Stevie was relieved it wasn't her turn this year, because for the second year in a row she would be having a quiet evening and an early night. She had no yen to stay up until midnight to wish a room full of strangers a happy New Year.

She shook her head at her own churlishness. It wasn't that she didn't wish others well—not at all. She'd promised herself when she left the home she'd so carefully created for her and Harrison and closed the door firmly behind her that she would focus on pleasing herself from now on. Some might say that was selfish. But for Stevie, it had become a matter of survival. She'd never considered herself a dependent type, but somehow, she'd allowed herself to change during her marriage into someone she hadn't recognized.

Chloe's death had been the first eye-opener, together with the harsh reality that her husband had been relieved when their daughter had drawn their last breath. He'd never wanted anything that wasn't perfect in his life. And he had no understanding of how to care about someone so different from what he considered normal. His death only a month later had been Stevie's second shock. Together with his family rallying around one another, but not her. Never her. She'd done everything the Reed family had ever expected or demanded of her, and when she most needed support, they'd left her stranded.

Yes, it was her own fault that she'd become so dependent on Harrison's every utterance. Convinced of the need to please him. Wanting to belong to a deeply traditional family. But now, looking back and understanding where her family had come from, the eccentricities they'd developed and the choices they'd made, it all made a perfect kind of sense. They'd been odd compared to the mainstream, but they'd been happy. She wanted that kind of happy, and it was up to her to create it. And for her—for now, at least, and maybe forever—that meant being on her own.

Stevie listened as a small group of guests departed Nickerson House in the party shuttle. No doubt they'd all be back in the wee small hours, loud and happy. With them gone, she could perform the turndown service early, collect wet bath linens, etcetera. She enjoyed providing the little touches that made a stay at Nickerson House a memorable one. She smiled in anticipation. She'd already planned a delightful evening for herself, starting with a body scrub and a long deep bath with a glass of wine or two, maybe a book. It would be heaven and she'd do it the minute she knew she was completely alone.

It only took forty minutes to check the guest rooms and complete her evening routine. She'd left Fletcher's room until last. Somehow, the act of turning down his sheets each night had become a bittersweet tradition during his stay. Since Christmas Day, he'd made sure to be out most days and several evenings as well. She wondered if he'd enjoy the party at the nearby hotel tonight. She was humming to herself quietly as she knocked gently on his door, called, "Housekeeping," and let herself in.

There was no one there, and she crossed quickly

to the windows and pulled the drapes closed, giving them an extra twitch to ensure they sat properly and then turned to the bed. She bent over the broad expanse and turned down the heavy top cover, ensuring the turndown was perfect and the sheets exposed were completely smooth before placing one of the handmade truffles from the specialty store in town on the pillow. *Time to check the bathroom now*, she thought, as she crossed the room. A light twist of the handle and the door was open and she was instantly enveloped in a wall of hot steam.

"Oh, I'm so sorry!" she exclaimed, backing away rapidly but not before she'd caught a glimpse of a gloriously naked and wet Fletcher Richmond in the frameless glass shower stall.

She only had time to see the wry grin that spread across his handsome features before she was out of the bathroom and, just as quickly, out of his suite. *Wet towels be damned*, she thought, as she hightailed it downstairs and into her office where she shut the door behind her and drew in a long, steadying breath.

She wouldn't think about him, she told herself sternly. Not his long, muscled thighs coated in a dusting of dark hair. Not his broad, strong shoulders or well-defined chest. Definitely not his belly, nor the way his hips had that all too enticing definition that drew the eye to— *Stop it! You won't think about him*, she repeated. But all the censures in the world didn't erase the memory of the perfection of him.

Of what seeing him did to her.

Longing poured through her, and she craved knowing what his skin would feel like if she stroked him, just so.

"Stop being stupid," she said out loud. "You don't want him."

Liar, a little voice answered in the back of her mind.

Okay, she reasoned as she sat behind her desk and looked at the list of guests checking out in the morning. *So, he's a very fine piece of work*, she admitted. It didn't mean anything that her body was now alight with a heat she couldn't ever remember feeling quite like this. Nor that her bra suddenly felt as if it was a size too small or that there was a throb deep inside her that demanded something she refused to acknowledge. *You're a healthy adult woman. You can be expected to react like this*, she told herself, staring unseeingly at her computer screen. *Plus, it's been a long time since you've enjoyed intimacy with anyone, let alone a man like Fletcher Richmond.*

His body had been hard planes of honed muscle. She'd always believed him to be on the slender, athletic side of male builds. Not an overly muscled type who probably spent more time at the gym than at work. But there was no denying the latent strength in his body. Every inch of him that she'd seen, and she'd seen a lot even in that embarrassing moment of realization that she wasn't alone, had been perfection.

And she wanted him.

She closed her eyes and groaned out loud, letting her head drop to her desk in defeat.

"Are you okay?"

Fletcher's voice from right in front of her desk made her bolt upright. She hadn't even heard him enter her office. A hot flush of awareness flooded her body as she forced herself to look at him, took in the damp hair and his fresh scent, courtesy of the bathroom accessories she took pride in providing. She'd never be able to smell that particular fragrance again and not think of him. Which meant changing her inventory or being tormented forever, she thought irrationally.

"Stevie?"

"What? Yes. Of course. I'm sorry I burst in on you like that. I thought you'd gone with the others. Did you want me to call the shuttle back for you?"

He smiled. "That's very kind, but I'm staying in tonight."

He was? *Damn.*

"Not going to paint the town red for the last night of the year?" she hinted, hopefully.

"No. I'm finishing this year the way I plan to start the next one. Quietly and with deliberation."

There was something about the way he'd said that last word that made her feel a frisson of foreboding.

"Deliberation, huh?"

"Exactly."

He put out his hand to her, and stupidly, she took it. Letting him pull her to her feet and toward him.

"Fletcher—" she started, but Fletcher had other ideas.

"No talking," he murmured.

And then he was kissing her. And it felt so right,

so perfect she let him do it, sank into it, reveled in it. For about ten seconds, until reason hit her with a cold, wet slap in the face and she pulled away.

"D-don't," she said. "P-please, don't."

He looked stricken. "I'm sorry. I thought we had something." He took a step back and then shook his head. "These past two weeks have given me two things. A chance to get my head in order and the torment of wanting you. I couldn't leave tomorrow without at least testing to see if you felt the same way. I apologize for overstepping the mark. I won't invade your personal space or time again."

He was gone an instant later, leaving her standing there, still speechless, still filled with the taste of him, the sensation of having been held in his arms. It was everything she'd dreamed of and not nearly enough at the same time. Damn it, what the heck was wrong with her? Why couldn't she accept what was there, what they both wanted, if the truth be told? Was she to be forever tormented by fear? Hadn't she spent this past year and a half regaining charge of herself and her needs and desires? Of course she had. And didn't she desire him?

She most definitely did.

So what did that leave? The answer had been right in front of her. That man, for one night. That's all it could be, and that would be enough, wouldn't it? It would have to be. Her choice. Her decision.

Stevie ran her hands through her hair and straightened her clothing. She couldn't believe she was going to do this, but she exited her office with just one destination in mind. A couple of minutes later, she was outside Fletcher's door, her heart hammering in her chest and her hand trembling as she raised it to knock.

He pulled the door open within seconds.

"Stevie?"

"I want you to invade my personal space. All of it. With deliberation."

Eight

Fletcher felt the air rush from his body as his brain processed Stevie's words. He stared at her, still unsure if he'd manifested his deepest desire or if she was really here. But then she stepped forward and pushed the door closed with her foot. And the second she put her arms around him and lifted her face to his, he knew, without doubt, that this was very, very real indeed.

He felt her lips graze his, at first tentatively, then with more confidence. It didn't take a rocket scientist to realize she had meant every word. Her lips were soft and he held back the urge to take control of their embrace and show her exactly how he felt right now. This was an exquisite gift, from her to him, and he wasn't about to mess it up. He let her explore his lips with her tongue, her teeth and parted his lips when she appeared to want more. Fletcher couldn't stifle the groan of need that ripped from his throat when she replaced her lips with the tips of her fingers, touching him so gently it was barely a touch at all.

He took her hand in his, held her fingers more firmly against his lips and kissed them before letting his tongue flick out to caress the crease between her fore and middle fingers. A tremor rippled through her, her eyes grew impossibly dark, and her cheeks lit with a flush of pink.

"I would like to do that to all of you," he said softly, barely daring to give voice to his fantasy in case he frightened her away.

"Me, too," she whispered in return. She pulled away slightly, and her voice grew firmer. "But I need to be clear. This is only for tonight. You leave in the morning, and I stay here. I don't want any more than that. So, let's take tonight and make it magical."

Her eyes were locked with his as she awaited his reply. When he nodded, she kissed him again, this time with more confidence, and this time he reciprocated in kind. Stevie tunneled her fingers through his hair, and he relished her touch. Relished the fact that the woman he'd been attracted to for years, the woman who had been forbidden to him was finally in his arms.

"Take me to bed, Fletcher," she demanded softly against his mouth.

He wasted no time in scooping her into his arms and walking to the four-poster where he'd dreamed of her every night for the past two weeks. He set her gently on the bed and his hands went immediately to his belt buckle to loosen it. It took him valuable seconds to disrobe before he could reach for her again. While he'd undressed, Stevie had removed her top and bra, exposing smooth, fair skin and breasts tipped with deep rose-pink nipples. Nipples that were taut and which made his mouth water, imagining how they'd feel against his tongue.

Why imagine it? he asked himself as he helped her wriggle out of her jeans and remove her panties and socks. She reached for him then, pulling him over her, silently urging him to cover her with his body. The sensation of skin on skin was sheer bliss, better than anything he'd experienced before. She was smooth and soft, and her entire body radiated a welcoming heat that he felt along his entire length. He bent his head and nuzzled her neck, inhaling her sweet scent and committing it to memory because he was nobody's fool. He knew that come morning, he had to return to his life in Norfolk. A life that didn't include Stevie Nickerson, even if he wanted it to. She'd made her feelings plain on the topic and he had to respect her wishes on that, no matter how many different ways he could imagine making a long-distance affair work. He had to take what he was offered and enjoy it. And he did.

Fletcher took his time exploring Stevie's body, enjoying the sounds of pleasure she made as he trailed his fingers along her shoulders, then down her arms before tracing back up again to follow the contours of her breasts. Goose bumps raised on her flesh as he did so, and beneath him, she squirmed, her hips pressing against him in silent entreaty.

"Do you like that?" he asked gently.

"So much," she gasped in reply.

A small smile played across his lips and he lowered his head to one breast and took her nipple in his mouth. He rolled the tightly bunched tip with his tongue. She jolted as if she'd received an electric shock.

"Still okay?" he murmured against her skin.

"So okay."

Ever the gentleman, Fletcher applied his attention to her other breast before kissing a trail across her rib cage and to her belly. Everything about her was so lush and feminine and so perfect, all at the same time. His fingers hovered over faint silver lines on her belly before his journey of discovery continued to her hips and upper thighs, particularly the patch of dark brown hair at her center. Her entire body grew taut as he played with her there, almost but not quite touching.

"Are you trying to torture me?" she asked, propping herself up on her elbows and eyeing him with dark eyes glazed with sensual hunger.

"Yes. Is it working?" he answered with a wicked grin as he let his fingertip touch her clitoris and press more firmly.

She groaned and dropped back onto the pillow. His face grew serious as he put all his attention to the task at hand. He wanted to make this good for her, so good it would forever remain memorable for them both. So many years he'd dreamed of having her in his bed, just like this. Pliant and accepting and demanding and giving. The yin and yang of lovemaking between two people who belonged together—even if it was only for one night.

Her sweet, musky scent teased him to delve deeper, and he did, kissing her and touching her until she writhed in pleasure. He savored the taste of her, the textures of her body. And when her legs stiffened and her body grew taut beneath his caresses, he gently coaxed her over the edge and into the oblivion of orgasm. He slowed his movements, gentled her with soft touches as he moved to lie face-to-face with her. Fine beads of perspiration dotted her chest, her upper lip, her forehead—as if she'd been in a fever of desire and the fever had now broken.

But it was only just beginning, he promised silently. He kissed her, stroking his tongue against hers, stoking the fire of their passion until he knew he could wait no longer. He already knew the bedroom came stocked with protection, and it took only a moment to ensure they were covered. Fletcher kissed Stevie again.

"Are you okay?" he asked.

"I'm better than okay," she answered with a smile. "Let me show you how much better."

She shifted then so that she straddled him. She skimmed her palms over his chest and shoulders before sliding her hands to his hips and then to his erection. Stevie guided him to her entrance, lifting herself to take him into her body.

"How's this for personal space?" she said as she lowered herself and took him fully inside her and clenched tightly around his length.

Fletcher was beyond speech. It was all he could do to hold back and not grab her by the hips and thrust until he took them through the barriers of normality and into pleasure so sublime that there'd be no beginning or ending between them. The temptation was strong—so strong. But he forced himself to remain passive while she teased him with her inner muscles and the tilt of her hips. He sensed the moment when it stopped being a game to her and welcomed the serious expression that took over her features. Welcomed, too, the movement of her body as she began to move to a rhythm that he couldn't help but meet with every glide of her hips.

And then he was incapable of thought, incapable of control as his climax tore through him with a powerful surge. He felt her body clench and pulse as she, too, joined him in total surrender to pleasure. She collapsed against him and he wrapped his arms around her, holding her to him, grounding them as their heart rates slowly, inexorably returned to normal.

Stevie pressed a kiss to his throat and he murmured an indistinct sound in response, still incapable of speech. Being with her like this was everything he'd ever dreamed of, and more. And he did not want it to end.

"That was pretty good for our first time," she said

against his chest before nipping lightly at one of his nipples.

The sensation of her teeth on his skin sent a shock of pleasure through him, and even while he was still inside her, he could feel his body begin to harden anew.

"Pretty good? It was way better than that," he eventually managed to growl.

"Oh, I think we can do better."

And in an instant, he was fully hard again. "Better, you say?" he challenged. "What just happened is going to take some beating, don't you think?"

"Oh, sure, but it's going to be fun trying, isn't it?"

He had no answer for that but to roll her onto her back and withdraw from the heat of her body.

"Give me a minute," he said. "I'll be right back and we'll see what we can do."

Stevie unashamedly watched him walk across the bedroom to the bathroom, admiring the long, lean lines of his back and the taut curves of his buttocks as he went. She stretched appreciatively against the sheets, every nerve ending in her body alive and attuned to each sensation as she thought about what they'd just shared. It had been, quite frankly, the best sex she'd ever had in her life and she felt incredibly proud that she'd taken the lead and come to Fletcher tonight.

And it would just be tonight. She knew he was leaving in the morning and she was good with that. She had her own mission to follow. Her own goals to achieve. They didn't include having a romantic interest in her life. She wanted to be able to focus 100 percent on her plans for the hotel without distraction. Still, as distractions went, Fletcher Richmond was certainly a very adept one, she thought with a satisfied smile spreading across her face.

Fletcher came back toward the bed and she couldn't ignore the very obvious presence of his arousal. As he joined her on the bed, she reached for him.

"Goodness," she said with a smile. "Is this for me?"

He laughed, making her smile broaden. She'd never laughed like this in the bedroom before. Never teased. Never scaled the heights Fletcher had taken her to. She was glad that if she only got to do this right once in her life, that it was with him.

"Yours to do with what you want," Fletcher said, letting one broad hand drift to her hips. "Tell me, what is it that you want?"

"Well," she said with a small shiver of delight. She'd never felt so bold talking about what she wanted. "First, I'd like to hold you. Really feel you and stroke you from tip to base and back again. I might need to do that a few times before I've had enough."

"I see, and then?" His voice had grown thick with desire, and a vein pulsed at his throat.

"Hmm, let's see. And then I think I'd like to trace the shape of you with my tongue. Just the tip at first and then with my lips and mouth as well. And after that, I want to taste you. All of you."

She pinned him with her eyes, letting him know

in no uncertain terms that she had every intention of following through on her words.

"That sounds like something I'd really enjoy," Fletcher said.

"I had better get on with it, then, don't you think?"

"By all means."

He stretched out beside her and tucked his hands under his head as she straddled his thighs and took his length in her hand. She loved the feel of him. The smooth, heated texture of his skin, the silkiness of the tip. She tightened her grip and began to slowly stroke him as she'd described. He groaned and his body tensed beneath her.

"Too much?" she asked softly, easing her grip.

"Too much and not enough," he said. "But don't stop."

She shifted a little farther down his legs so she could bend to him more easily and started to stroke him again before flicking her tongue out to tease the tip of his penis. He groaned again. But this time, she didn't stop and didn't ease up. Instead, she continued her onslaught, exactly as she'd described. She took his length fully in her mouth, her tongue teasing and twining around him, sucking gently and then with more pressure until she felt his hands in her hair. Without letting him go, she looked up, saw his glittering gaze as he lifted his head to watch her. She held his eyes with her own as she continued. With a final groan of surrender, he dropped his head and let her take him to a world of sensation where only pleasure reigned.

She slowed and eased her ministrations until she let him go entirely, and she shifted up his body until she lay with her head on his chest, listening to his heart race in the aftermath of his climax. She'd done that to him, she thought with a huge amount of pride. She'd given him the level of fulfilment he'd so unselfishly given her, and it felt so right to do so. Fletcher's arm curled around her waist, holding her to him firmly as if he couldn't bear to let her go, and eventually, they drifted off to sleep that way.

The sound of fireworks going off woke them both, and wrapped in a sheet, they rose and went to the bedroom window together to watch the display in town that heralded the start of a new year.

"Here's hoping it's a good one," Fletcher said, holding her close to his side.

"Yeah," Stevie agreed.

Fletcher tipped her face to his when the display finished and murmured, "Happy New Year," before kissing her deeply.

It was different from the way he'd kissed her before. More intense and as if there was more emotion behind it. She told herself to pull away, to end this idyll they'd shared, but perversely her body wouldn't let her. She gave herself over to his kiss and lifted her hands to his head, holding him there as if what they were doing now was the most important thing in the world.

When Fletcher lifted her into his arms, letting the sheet drop from around them, and took her back to the bed, she didn't protest. And when he sheathed himself again and entered her body in a long, slow stroke, she accepted him, welcomed him, let her body undulate to meet his every movement. They took their time together, caressing and kissing until the pressure inside each of them demanded release. And when release came, it rivaled both in intensity and delight the fireworks display they'd seen outside.

Fletcher dragged the covers over them, and they drifted off to sleep, legs still entwined, bodies still joined, as if it were the most natural thing in the world.

When morning began to filter through the windows, Stevie woke with a start. She hadn't meant to stay the entire night. Fletcher continued to sleep on, and she gently eased herself from his side, aware of a stickiness between her legs that hadn't been there before. She looked back at the bed and saw the spent condom lying on the sheets. They'd fallen asleep before Fletcher had taken care of it.

Terror struck her. Surely she couldn't fall pregnant from that, right? Fate wouldn't be so cruel. Ignoring her rapidly increasing heart rate, Stevie quickly donned her clothing and let herself out of his suite before heading to her own. There, she went straight to the bathroom and entered a scalding hot shower. She cleaned and scrubbed and lathered and repeated it all over again. She couldn't be pregnant. She just couldn't.

Nine

Six weeks later

"Happy Valentine's Day. You're pregnant. Congratulations," her doctor confirmed.

"No, that's not p—"

She was about to say possible, but she knew it was eminently possible no matter how much she wished it were otherwise. Her cycle had always been erratic, but she'd begun to recognize the signs of pregnancy a couple of weeks ago and had done her best to ignore them. But denial hadn't worked for her, and here she was. Facing her worst nightmare.

"I've had a baby before," she said to the doctor, her voice shaking. "Chloe was born with trisomy 18 and died four weeks later. What are the odds of that happening again?"

Her doctor assumed a deeply sympathetic expression. "I'm so sorry for your loss, Stevie. As you've probably been told before, genetic irregularities like that can't be predicted. But let me check my database quickly and see if I can offer you some reassurance."

He clicked his computer mouse a few times, typed in a few words, then turned the computer screen to face Stevie.

"As you can see here, there is a one percent chance of it occurring again. But trisomy 18 is rarely an inherited mutation. It is a duplication error as cells are forming. The odds are far higher that you'll have a normal, healthy pregnancy with a normal, healthy baby at the end."

"But there are no guarantees, right?" she asked bluntly.

He shook his head. "I'm sorry to say it, but no. Honestly, Stevie, I can't recommend anything to you right now but to focus on that ninety-nine percent chance that there will be nothing wrong with your baby. Considering what has happened, I would like to recommend counseling to work through your options."

She swallowed against the massive lump that had lodged in her throat. "No, I'll be okay. I just need to think about things."

"Okay, then. Well, if that's everything, let's get you booked in for a dating scan in a few weeks, and I'll write you a script for the supplements you'll need."

Stevie was out on the street, clutching the prescription before she realized what she was doing. Shock continued to reverberate through her mind. She didn't know what to do, where to turn. Aside from Penny and Cliff, she had no support system in place. If she did this, it would be completely on her own.

What about Fletcher? You must tell him.

Ice flowed through her veins. She dreaded relaying the news to him but accepted it would need to be sooner rather than later—but where did she start? How would she find the words to tell him? Yes, she had his number and his home address from the booking information he'd given at the hotel, but as to the actual words…? And how would he take the news?

This wasn't the kind of information one shared with a phone call. She had to see him. She had a presentation to make in Virginia Beach, about half an hour from Norfolk, later in the week. She was using her concept drawings to pitch to a large conglomerate with an eye to securing their business for executive wellness spa getaways for their key staff. With the down payment from the contract, she'd easily be able to meet the increase in payments for the loan extension she'd applied for after all those weeks of gathering figures and data for the bank. Maybe she could see Fletcher while she was there. Kill two birds with one stone, so to speak.

When she'd initially made the reservations, before knowing she was pregnant, Stevie had been tempted to stop by to see Fletcher. To see if the spark between them was as strong as she remembered. But she reminded herself they lived in two different worlds. She wouldn't leave Asheville, and he couldn't leave Norfolk. And it wasn't worth having an occasional one-night stand. But now they might be forced into a relationship after all.

Stevie filled her script and drove home to Nickerson House. She avoided seeing Penny and fielding any questions that might arise and took the main stairs to the next level and went and hid in her room. Being pregnant would be hard work on her own— she'd been exhausted and anemic through her first pregnancy—but she refused to give up on her dreams of expanding the hotel's accommodation and services. After all, sleep was overrated, right? She chuckled, but the sound lacked any level of humor. She had no illusions. This was going to be tough. She needed to create a plan of how she would cope with everything. First up, she had to tell Fletcher.

The presentation had gone extremely well and Stevie felt buoyed with enthusiasm. It had been a while since she'd done anything like that in a corporate environment, but the moment she put on her suit and heels in her hotel room, she'd felt as if she'd armored herself for what she had to do. She had her data, her notes and her presentation down pat, and it had shown in the feedback and questions she'd gotten. While there was no contract yet, she was very confident she'd be inking one soon with a view to providing the service during the summer of next year. Which left only one more thing to do.

See Fletcher Richmond.

She'd done her homework and she knew where he worked. After leaving the presentation, she had called ahead and left a message she'd be by later. She hoped he was in the office today and free to see her. No problem if not, she'd told herself in a cowardly fashion. If he wasn't there today, she'd try him this evening, provided she hadn't thoroughly lost her nerve by then.

She took a cab to the imposing building flagged with Richmond Construction's logo. After she arrived, she stood on the sidewalk staring at the entrance for a few minutes before drawing in a deep breath and entering the building. A directory inside said the company's main offices were on the top floor. The ride in the elevator went far too quickly for her liking, because before she knew it, she was entering the lobby. A receptionist smiled a welcome.

"Good afternoon. May I help you?"

"I'm Stevie Nickerson. I'd like to see Mr. Richmond."

"We have two Mr. Richmonds. Which one do you wish to see?"

"Fletcher. Fletcher Richmond."

Stevie's mouth went dry just saying his name. How on earth was she going to tell him about the baby?

"Do you have an appointment?" the receptionist asked.

"I did mention I was stopping by later, but I am early."

"I'm sorry, Ms. Nickerson. Mr. Fletcher didn't confirm an appointment, perhaps—"

Another woman who had entered reception right behind her stepped up to the front desk. "I can take Ms. Nickerson to see Fletcher. I know he's free right now."

"But she has no appointment."

"It's okay. He won't mind. Come with me," the newcomer said.

Stevie eyed her dubiously. She looked slightly familiar, but she couldn't quite place why. Then it clicked. This must be Lisa Richmond, Fletcher's sister, the youngest sibling.

"Thank you. I appreciate it," she said carefully.

"No problem. I'm Lisa, Fletcher's sister. His office is along this corridor."

Lisa led the way without any further comment and gave a short knock on the door to Fletcher's office before swinging it open.

"You have a visitor," she announced before stepping back to usher Stevie in.

Stevie took one step, then another until she was staring at a very different Fletcher Richmond from the man she'd last seen New Year's Day. This was Fletcher in his natural setting. Gone were the jeans and the long-sleeved T-shirts and sweaters. In their place was a bespoke suit with a silk tie and pristine white business shirt. Not a hair was out of place and not a whisker of the stubble she'd grown used to was to be seen.

"Stevie? I just got your message. I didn't expect

to see you again," he started as he rose from behind his desk.

"I'm pregnant," she blurted out. All her careful plans, all her ideas about discussing this rationally had just flown out the window at the sight of Fletcher standing before her. Somehow, seeing him again—looking like a polished stranger—brought out the emotion and fear and the terror she had tried to tamp down.

Fletcher's eyes widened, then flicked to over Stevie's shoulder.

"I'll just close the door on my way out, shall I?" Lisa said from behind her.

Fletcher crossed the distance between his desk to where Stevie was standing shaking in her high-heels.

"Come, sit," he said, guiding her gently to a sofa.

She gratefully sank onto the seat and closed her eyes, feeling the depression of the cushion as Fletcher sat beside her. He put one arm around her shoulders and pulled her against him.

"You're shaking like a leaf. Can I get you anything?"

"No, I'm fine. I'm sorry I just came out with it. I didn't quite know how to tell you."

He chuckled. "Well, you've told me all right. Are you sure? Of course you are. You wouldn't have traveled this distance to tell me if you weren't."

"I didn't want to tell you over the phone. I thought it best to talk face-to-face. Get things clear."

She felt him stiffen beside her.

"Get things clear?" he asked coolly. "What things?"

"I don't know. I don't know what I want to do next. There's so much to think about."

"Surely that's something we can tackle together, right? It's our baby."

As he said the words, Fletcher felt the enormity of them begin to sink in. He'd been about to be a father once before, back when he was a teenager and his girlfriend, Laura, had become pregnant. Her parents had stepped in and made it clear he had no choice in what happened after that. He wasn't allowed to see or communicate with Laura in any way. After matters had been "taken care of," she and her family had moved to another state. He never heard from her again and he'd been heartbroken. His parents had been high school sweethearts. He had been the reason they'd gotten married, even if the marriage had turned out to be null and void because his mom had forged her parents' permission. But even so, they'd made their relationship work, and they'd raised him and subsequently his brother and sister in a loving family home.

To this day, he remained conflicted about not having a say in what happened to his child, and he'd mourned that baby something fierce. Still did. But now he was presented with another unexpected pregnancy, and as an adult, he knew no one would be able to deny his input into the situation. Already, he felt a sharp need to protect his unborn child and its mother.

He could fix this. He could use the connection he had with Stevie and take care of his new family. He could do this in the right way. No lies like his parents had told, no exclusion like Laura's family had created. And maybe they could work toward building a future together as a family.

"We can get married," he said.

"I beg your pardon?" Stevie was looking at him in shock. He felt the same shock at his words.

"It makes sense. We'll get married. I can provide for you and the baby. You'll want for nothing. I won't stand back and let you take all the responsibility. This is something we'll do together, Stevie."

"I'm not marrying you, Fletcher. Look, I felt an obligation to tell you that I'm carrying your child. I only found out earlier this week, and I'm still coming to terms with it myself. I don't know how involved I want you to be."

"How involved *you* want me to be? You don't get a choice in that, Stevie. This is my baby, too."

"I'm not denying it, but I do have a choice about what happens next. Don't try to browbeat me or guilt me into something I don't want. I won't live through that again."

She sounded adamant. Far stronger than she had a moment ago. He wasn't used to failure, but for now, he was prepared to leave it and decided to take a different tack.

"How did it happen, anyway? We used protection."

"Yes, but when we fell asleep after the fireworks, you were still inside me."

Just thinking about the perfection of the intimacy they'd shared and how it had felt to fall asleep with her in his arms sent a powerful surge of longing through his body. It had been nice to have that break. But then her words sank in and, with them, the reality that he'd let her down. He hadn't taken care of her as he ought to have.

"I'm sorry," he said softly. "I should have been more careful."

She shook her head. "It's happened. We have to deal with it."

"Together, we will."

She looked him directly in the eyes. "Don't push me, Fletcher. This is my body we're talking about. My life."

"And my child, too. Don't forget that."

"How could I? Honestly, this is the worst thing that could have happened to me. Can't you understand that? What if something goes wrong? What then?"

"Why would anything go wrong?" he demanded.

"You have no idea," she said sadly, shaking her head. "Look, I can't talk about this right now. I'm going back to my hotel."

"Where are you staying? Maybe I can take you?"

She told him the name of the hotel and shook her head at his offer.

"No, I'll take a cab. I'm heading home in the morning. I just wanted you to know, and you do. I'll be in touch when I've got things figured out."

He watched, helpless, as she rose and walked out of his office. Everything in him urged him to race ahead of her, to coax her back and to sit her down and talk to her until she saw his side of things. But if he understood only one thing about Stevie, it was that doing something like that would guarantee that she wouldn't listen to him again. She would have no hesitation in cutting him out of this altogether if he acted like he was in charge of her future. And, slowly, he began to understand why she was so opposed to marriage.

Harrison hadn't been the kind of man to listen. He had always been the leader, never the follower. It was always his way or the highway. That was okay when you were just buddies and happy to keep the status quo because you knew that when it counted, you went your own way. But if you were married to him? That would be an entirely different kettle of fish, wouldn't it? If Stevie's marriage had been a succession of moments where her wishes had never been considered, and he suspected that was likely the case, then he could begin to understand how she might have lost her sense of self and why she was prepared to fight so hard to preserve that now.

And, more to the point, if he wanted to be a part of her life and their baby's, he had to figure out how to communicate with her in a way that would show he'd do whatever it took to keep her and the baby safe and well.

His office door opened again. He looked up hopefully, expecting Stevie's return to reopen their discussion.

"Well, that was interesting," Lisa said without disguising her obvious interest in what she'd overhead before leaving the office a short while ago. "Care to fill me in?"

"Not particularly," Fletcher said. "At least, not now."

"I'm assuming it's your baby she's expecting."

He went and sat behind his desk. "Not now, Lisa. I don't want to talk about it."

His sister shrugged. "You're going to have to talk about it eventually, Fletch. I'll be here with an ear when you're ready."

When he didn't respond, she left the office, closing the door again behind her. Fletcher dropped his head in his hands and groaned. Somehow, he had to find a way to get it through to Stevie that he wasn't the bad guy here. He'd do whatever it took, and for however long it was necessary, so that she understood. But one thing he wouldn't do was simply sit back and wait quietly. Any decisions made about their baby would be made by them together. He just had to get her to see that, too.

Ten

Stevie got out of the shower in her hotel room and wrapped herself in the complementary toweling robe. She was shattered. It had been a long drive to Virginia Beach yesterday, with all the associated tension that the presentation had brought her, but the emotional toll of telling Fletcher of her pregnancy had left her totally drained.

She should have anticipated him saying what he had, but even so, hearing it had just reminded her so much of her previous life and her lack of choices then. She accepted that had been her own fault because she'd found it easier to give in than to make a stand for what she thought or felt, because she hadn't wanted to rock the boat. And she'd let her late husband's personality overwhelm hers to the point where she'd barely been able to make a single major decision without running it by him first.

She supposed that had, in part, been because her grandmother had been a woman with a big personality and very strong ideas about things. A quiet child, Stevie hadn't wanted to rock the boat at home, either. Growing up without her parents meant she hadn't wanted anything to happen to upset the security of her world. When she met Harrison, he'd represented a new form of security for her. Financial as well as emotional. Some might have seen the way he acted as a form of abuse, but she knew she'd let him walk all over her—she'd wanted to be taken care of even if it meant relinquishing every last scrap of independence. It was only after Chloe was born that her need to assert herself, for both her and her baby daughter, had arisen. And the pushback from her husband had been huge.

They'd argued the day he went flying. He'd told her it was time for her to get on with her life and that he was glad Chloe had died because they were no longer encumbered with what he considered a defective child. Stevie had lashed out with harsh words, telling him exactly where he could shove his unspeakably vile attitude to his own flesh and blood. Those words had hung in the air between them as he coldly departed for the airfield—the last words she'd ever say to him. She'd struggled with that afterward, but she'd eventually made her peace once she returned home to Asheville and laid her daughter's ashes to rest in the Nickerson family plot.

Now she was making her own decisions and choices, for better or worse. And it felt good to be back in control. Yes, this pregnancy had thrown her for a loop and would put a serious dent in her plans, but with the right support and a solid business footing going forward, she'd manage it all. She knew she would. She just needed that corporate account for guaranteed income and the extension on her bank loan for everything to fall into place perfectly.

Stevie selected a dress and boots to wear for dinner here in the hotel. She'd considered room service but was always curious about hotel menus and service levels wherever she went, so she headed downstairs for her evening meal. She was making her way across the lobby toward the restaurant when she was arrested by the sight of Fletcher Richmond at the concierge desk. She walked up to him.

"Fletcher? What are you doing here?"

He spun around in response. She looked at his face and noted the gray cast to his skin and the tightness around his mouth and eyes. Had she done this to him with the news of their pregnancy? He looked terrible.

"Stevie, thank goodness. I really wanted to talk before you went back to Asheville."

"I'm just heading in for some dinner. Did you want to join me?"

"I'd love to," he said.

Once they were seated and had placed their orders, Fletcher wasted no further time in speaking what was clearly weighing heavily on his mind.

"Stevie, I want to apologize for my reaction back

in the office earlier today. Your news sent me off-kilter and I reacted badly, saying stuff without thinking it through or respecting your side of things."

She nodded slowly. "Thank you, I accept your apology. But while I do appreciate that you've gone to this effort to see me, it doesn't change anything. I'm not interested in marriage, Fletcher."

"Would you at least hear me out?" he asked.

"You're here at my dinner table, aren't you?" she pointed out.

He sighed. "Look, I'm sorry. It's been hard for my family this past year and it's left me feeling adrift. Discovering my parents' marriage was invalid came as a shock to all of us. Initially, I didn't think it mattered, but now I realize that everything about the foundation of my world, my family, was based on a carefully constructed series of lies. I know that when it comes to my child, I want there to be a solid foundation for us. I grew up with my parents together but my father away for half the time, never sure if he'd be around for important things in my life. I don't want my child to live like that. I want to be there as a full-time, hands-on father. I don't want weekend visitations and alternate holidays. I want my kid to grow up with two parents who have a commitment to one another. I want to ensure our child grows up with the utmost stability and honesty as the backbone to our family. It's not too much to ask, is it?"

Stevie began to speak but stopped as the waiter brought the first course and set it at the table. She picked up her fork and began to play with her food, choosing her words carefully before answering.

"Look, I appreciate you've had a shock with your family, but you have to realize how archaic your attitude is. Kids have been raised for decades in single-parent homes and shifting between single-parent homes without lifelong emotional scars."

"I get that, and I know I'm probably beating a worn-out drum here, but it's important to me to be an active part of the decisions around raising my kid. I respect your standpoint, I really do, but the baby is mine also, and don't I deserve some say in how they're raised and to be an equal contributor to their upbringing? You must agree that would be easier if we were together."

"But why would it be better for our child if we're not in love? That is why people get married, isn't it? Because they are, or believe they are, in love? Trust me, marriage isn't the answer to everything. I should know," she finished bitterly.

"Look, I see what you're saying, but I believe that if we went into this, eyes wide open about our expectations, there's no reason why it couldn't work out. Nor is there any reason we wouldn't come to love one another in time. We'd be bonded by our child, our own flesh and blood. What stronger connection could a couple have?"

She stared at her plate. She'd believed a child would bond a couple together, but it didn't always happen that way. Sometimes a baby drove a wedge between a couple that created an impassable void.

"Look, Stevie, if you'll let me, I can help you with whatever you need—help with the baby, help with the hotel—physically, financially, you name it and it's done."

"A baby is a full-time commitment, you know that don't you? Night and day—no matter what. And what if something is wrong with the baby? What then?"

She couldn't help it. It had to be said. From the stricken look on Fletcher's face, he hadn't been expecting her challenge to his suggestion. He painted such a simple picture, without considering for one minute that things might not be quite so perfect after all.

She'd thought about waiting to tell Fletcher until the four-month scan. They'd likely know then if the baby had trisomy 18. But what if there was some other problem? How would he deal with that? And, worse, what if their child died?

Emotion overwhelmed her, and she let her fork drop to her plate. The last thing she wanted to do was cry in front of him—to appear weak. She was in charge of her life and wouldn't be coerced into agreeing to anything she didn't want.

"I'm sorry. I can't do this now."

"Stevie, you can't keep walking away from me when our conversation takes a turn you don't like. At some point, you will need to face up to the reality that we will be parents together."

She ignored him, as she'd become so adept at doing. She couldn't make the big decisions he was demanding right now. She needed space, so she would take as much as she needed. "The meal is charged to my room. Please stay and enjoy your food. We can discuss this further some other time."

She rose quickly to her feet and all but ran to the elevator lobby and was relieved to catch one heading up. A quick glance over her shoulder showed her that Fletcher had followed, but as the doors to the elevator slid closed, she saw the resignation on his face. She knew she'd probably hurt him, but she couldn't just accept his offer on face value and she'd meant it when she'd said she didn't want to marry again. What would it take for him to understand that? Marriage wasn't a cure-all, and it certainly wasn't a business transaction.

By the end of the week, Fletcher was seething with frustration. He'd tried to reach Stevie but after leaving a couple of messages for her and sending an email that remained unanswered he accepted he needed to back off for a while. And it wasn't as if he didn't have enough work on his plate at the office, either. One of their regular suppliers had unexpectedly closed their doors and filed for bankruptcy, leaving them in the lurch for finishing a project on time for a major client. If they were late, the penalties would be huge and Richmond Construction would take a massive hit. He'd worked late every night so his assistant could clear his schedule for Friday afternoon to allow him to drive to the mountains. If the mountain wouldn't return his calls, then he'd have to go visit the mountain. He arrived at Nickerson House in the early evening. It had rained heavily for most of the journey, and he was bone weary with concentration and the effects of a demanding week in the office.

He entered by the main door and rang the small brass bell at reception, then waited. It wasn't long before he heard quick footsteps coming from the hallway that led to the kitchen. Footsteps that slowed and began to lag as Stevie recognized who awaited her.

"Stevie," he said by way of greeting.

"Fletcher, I wasn't expecting you," she said, a flush of color staining her cheeks.

His eyes riveted on her darker ones, and he noted the way her pupils enlarged and her nostrils flared ever so slightly. Her lips parted on an indrawn breath, making her chest rise and fall. Her hair was loose in a glorious tumble of wavy curls that spread over her shoulders and tempted him to bend his head and inhale the scents surrounding her. He pushed all his senses into a box where they wouldn't distract him or lead him into trouble and focused instead on the purpose of his journey.

"No, I imagine that since you couldn't bring yourself to return my calls or answer my emails that you wouldn't have been expecting me, but here I am. Can we finish our discussion, please?"

"You came all this way just to do that?"

"It was kind of hard to do when you refused to communicate with me."

"I hope you're not expecting to stay here, we're—"

"Full up?" he said with a sardonic lift of his brow.

"I expected that to be the case when you saw me. I'll stay at one of the chain hotels in town."

"Oh? Which one?"

"Does it matter? I'm here now, and if you could spare an hour or so, maybe we could talk this out? Have you eaten?"

"I was just about to eat when you rang the bell."

He waited for the invitation to join her, but it wasn't forthcoming. Always a believer that there were times you got a better result by remaining silent than by speaking unnecessarily, he simply continued to stare at her. Eventually, Stevie heaved a huge sigh.

"Okay, fine. Since you've come all this way, you may as well join me."

Tempted to remark on her gracious invitation, he reminded himself that her company was what he sought, not to piss her off, so he kept his response simple.

"Thanks. I appreciate it."

"Follow me," she said as she turned and headed back to the kitchen and, once there, gestured for him to take a seat.

"No Penny today?" he observed.

"She took dinner home to share with Cliff. He's on an early shift this week."

He watched as she carved slices of roast beef and put them on his plate together with a generous serving of mashed potatoes and steamed green beans, then poured an even more generous serving of rich dark gravy over it all.

"There," she said plonking the plate in front of him. "I hope you like gravy."

"I love gravy," he said appreciatively. "And I can't remember the last time I had mashed potatoes."

He waited for her to pick up her fork and begin to eat before he tasted his meal. As simple as it was, it tasted heavenly and he said as much.

"Penny is a wizard in the kitchen," Stevie acknowledged. "Now, you want to talk?"

"I do. I wondered if you had time to think about my suggestion."

"I have."

"And?" he prompted when she offered no further information.

"I will not marry you. It's not just you, Fletcher. I don't ever want to marry again."

"Can you tell me why?"

"I lost my sense of self when I married Harrison, and I allowed him to mold me into what he wanted, every step of the way. I never pushed back. I never had a voice. I let that happen and I won't let it happen again."

"You say you let that happen, but I know how persuasive he could be. And, if you won't be offended by my saying this, manipulative, too."

"When he told me I was weak and needed him, even though it initially felt wrong, I agreed to everything he said. Everything. Anyway," she said with a sharp gesture of her hand, "that's all in the past. I'm my best version of me now. A strong me. A decisive me. A successful me. I don't need any man to complete me or to rule me or make decisions for me."

Fletcher nodded as her words hit home. "I respect that, Stevie, and you have done an incredible job with Nickerson House, but aren't you worried how you'll cope with all your duties and a newborn?"

"I will deal with it as and when the situation arises. I can always take on temp help, and if I get the retreat contract, I'll be able to bring on a couple of part-timers or a full-time staff member to fill in when I'm unable to be on duty."

"And if you don't win the retreat contract?"

"There are other firms to pitch to, your own for example," she said defiantly. "And, if no one takes up the contract offer, then I won't exactly be slammed for business, and Penny and Elsa and I will muddle on as we always have done in the past."

"Is that what you want? To muddle on?" He couldn't help the wry twist of his mouth as he said the words.

"Like I said, Fletcher. My choice, my decision to make. No one else's."

He nodded again and put his hands up in surrender. "Okay, I'm sorry. You have very clearly thought all this through and I respect you for that. Immensely, I might add. But have you never craved the intimacy that being a part of a couple can bring? The togetherness, the sharing of ideas, the melding of minds… and bodies."

Her breathing hitched, and her cheeks flared with color. He felt his own body heat in response, felt need for her—even if only to hold her—curl insidiously through his body. He'd promised himself he'd keep his attraction to her under control. To try to keep this meeting on a more professional footing, if only to show her he meant business and that his primary goal was to give her support.

"It's overrated," she said, dropping her gaze to her plate and pushing her dinner around with her fork. "Why is this all so important to you, anyway? A lot of men would just want to throw money at the problem—" she made air quotes with her fingers on the last word "—and be grateful they don't have to be hands-on."

"I am not 'a lot of men.' And I have a lot of reasons for wanting to be in my child's life. To be a good dad, preferably married to the mother of my baby."

"So, if these reasons are so important, why don't you share them with me instead of trying to browbeat me into submitting to what you want?"

His instant refusal of her suggestion that he was, in a way, bullying her, caught in his throat. She was right, he had been browbeating her. He'd heard her speak, but had he actually listened to a word she'd said? Really and truly listened?

"I'm sorry, Stevie. I've never had to fight for what I want this hard before."

She snorted an inelegant sound of derision. "What? Never?"

"There was this one time, but I lost, badly. It made me determined never to lose again."

"You expect me to believe the great Fletcher Richmond actually lost at something?"

"Watch it there. You'll have me thinking you admire me or something."

"Or something. Give it up, Fletcher. What happened?"

He took a moment to get his thoughts in order. It had been a long time since he'd allowed himself to talk to anyone about this. Even all these years later, the pain was so raw and blinding that he could already feel the knot of emotion that tightened his gut. He hated talking about this, hated thinking about it because thinking about it reminded him of how helpless he'd been in the face of the decisions being made by people who kept telling him they were only doing the right thing.

He drew in a deep breath and concentrated on speaking without losing control of the emotions that bubbled all too close to the surface. "I was going to be a father once. But I never had a chance."

Eleven

If he'd have hit her over the head with a cast-iron pan, Stevie knew she wouldn't have been more stunned than she was at this moment. Words failed her. He'd lost a child? Compassion and recognition of his loss flooded her and filled her eyes with unshed tears. She ached to reach across the table and take his hand, to offer him some comfort somehow. But she could see her touch wouldn't be welcome. He was lost in the agony of the past. A past he clearly kept buried deep inside.

"Fletcher, I'm so sorry," she finally managed through frozen lips. "I had no idea."

"It wasn't exactly bandied about for public knowledge and by the time I started college I'd learned how to keep it hidden."

"Can you tell me what happened? Obviously, I'd understand if you'd rather not talk about it."

"No, I've started now, and it's important to me that you know. She was my high school sweetheart. We had big plans for our future together, but when we discovered she was pregnant, everything changed."

Stevie did some quick mental calculations. "You were what? About eighteen?"

"Seventeen. Maybe if it had happened a year later, we would have had more say in the matter. Anyway, as it was, we didn't. Her parents refused to discuss the matter with mine. Said that Laura was their daughter, their responsibility, and that they'd take care of things."

The bitterness in his tone gave Stevie a clearer insight into what probably happened next. Fletcher continued, "For months I tried to see her, but they wouldn't let me in the door. They'd confiscated her phone so I couldn't call her or text. Even her friends were told to block me. Though one girlfriend did tell me that Laura wanted me to take her away, that she wanted us to keep the baby. But she wasn't at school anymore, and when I went around to their house, her parents threatened to call the police on me."

"That had to have been so hard for you," she said softly.

"It was nothing compared to discovering a week later that they'd moved away. I had no idea where and no way of contacting Laura. It was months before I learned what had happened. One of her girlfriends finally took pity on me and told me her family had forced her to agree to give up our child for adoption and had taken her away to start a new life. She'd been categorically told that they would withdraw all financial support for her dreams for college if she made any attempt to contact me or tell me about the baby. Hell, I didn't even know if it was a boy or a girl. My dad was away when I got the news and Mom told me never to mention it again." He made a sound halfway between a growl and a sigh. "When I was able, I hired a private detective to find out what he could. I'd had a son but the adoption records were sealed. I only hope that one day, maybe, my boy will want to know who his birth father is. But in the meantime, I have nothing of him. And he has nothing of me, either."

Stevie felt the suppressed anger he still bore for his dad for not being there when he needed his support and guidance, not to mention the grief he still felt over not having any access to his son, but there was nothing she could say that would make it better. Instead, she got up and cleared their plates; both of them had clearly lost interest in eating. She started to make him a coffee and a cup of tea for herself. When the drinks were ready, she sat at the table. Fletcher was as still as a statue, his hands on the scarred wooden surface in front of him, his eyes fixed on his hands. He flinched as if he'd been jerked out of a private reverie that he couldn't share with anyone else when she pushed his mug of coffee toward him.

"Again, Fletcher, I am so deeply sorry for what you went through. I know what it feels like to lose a child. It's soul destroying."

"I never knew you and Harrison lost a baby until his funeral when she was mentioned in his eulogy. That must have been devastating for both of you. I know, for myself, there's not a day I don't think about my boy. Maybe knowing my story will help to explain why our child is so important to me and why I need to be a part of their life."

"I do. I understand. Absolutely. In fact, to be totally honest with you, having another baby terrifies me because I know things can go horribly wrong. Look, I promise I'll give it more thought, but Fletcher, I truly don't see how things could work with us living four hundred miles apart."

"We'll make it work. I know we can if we're on the same page."

He meant if she agreed to his demands, she thought darkly before shaking the uncharitable idea loose from her mind. He wasn't her late husband, and despite everything she'd thought to the contrary, Fletcher Richmond appeared to be a decent man. Sure, he was happy to steamroll ahead to get what he wanted and he had good reason to, from what she'd discovered from him tonight, but she knew that essentially he wanted to find a solution that would work for them both. In itself, that was a promising position. However, the reality wouldn't change. His family business was in Norfolk, Virginia, and her entire world was here in Asheville, North Carolina.

"We can talk more in the morning, and you need to get your accommodation sorted out. Unless…"

Fletcher looked up. "Unless?"

Stevie closed her eyes a moment before answering him. "Unless you'd like to take a room here for the night?"

He did that thing with his eyebrow. "I thought you were full."

"I might have stretched the truth a little. Your previous suite is available, if you want it."

"Are you sure? I wouldn't want to put you out."

"Fletcher, just take the room, okay?" she answered with a generous portion of irritation thrown in.

"Thank you. I'm grateful. And we'll talk more in the morning? Over breakfast?"

"Sure, I need to see some of our guests to the ski slope shuttle, but after that I'm all yours."

He looked at her then and she immediately regretted her choice of words. All his? What would he do if she were all his? Would there be a repeat of the last time he stayed here, of his last night? A demanding curl of need wound through her body, setting every nerve ending on fire. She tore her gaze from his. They couldn't go down that path again; it would be madness. No matter how attracted she was to him physically, it didn't change her resolve to remain independent, and the reality was, with the way she felt about Fletcher now, she would all too easily cave to wanting to please him and live life his way.

By morning, she had strengthened her resolve. When she'd returned from taking her guests to meet the shuttle, she felt that she was resilient enough to resist Fletcher no matter how compelling his argument. *Sure you are*, a snaky little voice at the back of her mind jeered. *Just like you were the last time*. Stevie shook her head. No, she would not give into negative self-talk. That was an all too slippery slope.

She pulled up her vehicle at the back of the house and let herself into the kitchen. She was surprised to see Fletcher at the stove, being coached by Penny on making a Spanish omelet. He looked totally at home there as he added thinly sliced potatoes to a skillet with hot oil.

"That's all I put in it? Potatoes? What about onion? What about red pepper?" he asked as he turned to crack eggs into a bowl and began whisking them as if they'd personally offended him.

"I said whisk the eggs, not beat them to next century," Penny said with a chuckle. "Here, add a generous pinch of salt to that. Now, as to your question, the traditional tortilla Espanola, or Spanish omelet, is just that—potato and egg. Of course, you can make it whatever you want, and if you add sliced onions to the frying potato slices—it does help sweeten the dish—that's your choice. Red pepper, too. Cooking is all about choices. It's fun."

"Penny, I didn't know we expected our guests to cook their own breakfasts," Stevie said as she put her keys in a bowl on the table and hooked her handbag up by the door.

"I thought it might be a good opportunity for us to test out my trial menu for when we start the Cook Your Own gourmet weekends," Penny said without a hint of guilt. "Especially seeing as it was Fletcher's idea."

Fletcher gave Penny a quick grin. "I'm glad to hear you decided to give that a go. You could build up a big following, especially if each weekend follows a specific theme."

"We haven't actually decided on going ahead with that yet," Stevie said with a glare in Penny's direction. "It's still under discussion."

"Can't talk it to death forever," Penny said matter-of-factly. "It's a good idea, but if it doesn't work out, then we ditch it. No harm, no foul. All our costs would be covered anyway."

"But it's not my end goal," Stevie pointed out.

"But it might be a great way to get there. Besides, small business needs to be flexible to survive in this financial climate," Penny replied calmly.

She shifted her attention to what Fletcher was doing at the stove and guided him to drain off some of the oil from the skillet before adding the potatoes to the egg mixture, stirring them up and returning them to the pan.

"Normally, we'd let the egg-and-potato mixture rest a while before putting it in the pan," Penny pointed out. "But I guess you're hungry and would rather not wait?"

In response to his agreement, she continued to give him instructions on cooking, then flipping the omelet, while she chopped slices of chorizo sausage and browned them in another pan. After he'd slid the omelet onto a platter, Penny deftly sliced it up and put portions on two warmed plates and loaded them with the chorizo, adding tomato salsa on the side.

"There you are. Breakfast! Enjoy!"

"You're not eating with us?" Fletcher asked.

"No, I have some work in the greenhouse to do. Best I leave you two to it."

Stevie watched Penny shrug into her jacket and head out the back door.

"What was that about?" she asked.

"I told her we were going to talk today."

Stevie felt a rush of anger. She wasn't ready for everyone to know what was happening just yet. It was far too early, her pregnancy far too vulnerable. Hell, she was too vulnerable.

"What exactly did you say? I haven't told her I'm pregnant yet. You didn't tell her, did you?" she demanded.

"No, of course I wouldn't betray your confidence like that."

Stevie felt all the anger rush out of her. "I'm sorry I jumped to conclusions."

"Seems to me you're carrying an awful lot on those slender shoulders of yours. You can share the load, you know."

"It's my business, Fletcher. You of all people should understand how important it is to keep things under control."

"Control, yes. Strangulation, no."

And, boom, the anger was back again. "I beg your pardon?"

"Part of being a good boss is knowing when to

delegate. She's good at what she does—better than good. The gourmet-cooking weekends have her really excited. Why not give her free rein on them? After all, as she said, you have nothing to lose."

"I'll give it due consideration in my own good time."

"Of course you will," he said, holding out her chair and gesturing for her to sit. "We should eat this before it gets cold."

Begrudgingly, she sat, but her ill humor passed the moment she tasted breakfast. "Mmm, this is good," she said. "What made you ask Penny to show you?"

He nodded in acknowledgement as he tasted the meal himself and added a little more cracked pepper.

"I get bored with the same old dishes all the time."

"I don't get a chance to get bored with Penny here," she admitted with a rueful smile. "Is it hard being on your own, or do you have a revolving door of companions to keep you entertained?"

It was none of her business whether he kept a string of girlfriends, but if he were going to be a part of their baby's life, she wanted someone with stability—someone who'd be a good role model.

"Stevie, there hasn't been anyone since Tiffany left me when my dad died, and we were together for two years before that."

She felt her body ease up a little of the tension she was carrying. He could have teased her, made her feel uncomfortable for her nosiness into his personal life. But he hadn't. She needed to learn to lighten up and respect the fact that he was a decent guy.

"Look," he continued, "I can understand that you're nervous about making changes to your life all over again. After all, in the past couple of years, you've done a lot, what with being widowed and coming to terms with your grief, then moving back here. But you're adaptable, too. You are an incredibly strong and clever woman—resourceful, too. And you're going to be a magnificent mom. You deserve to be happy again."

"I am happy now."

"Truly happy, Stevie? I see the shadows in your eyes when you think no one is looking. You need to cut yourself some slack. You're going to have to when the baby comes anyway."

"And that's where you see yourself fitting in? Taking up that slack you mentioned? Helping with the baby so I can keep up with my professional obligations?"

"If you'll let me, yeah."

"And what about your professional obligations, Fletcher? My kid deserves more than just a weekend or a vacation parent."

"I know that."

"Then, what will happen? You'll relocate Richmond Construction to Asheville, or do you expect me to move to Norfolk?" she asked scathingly.

"These are things we need to work out."

Penny chose that moment to return through the back door. Stevie knew she could feel the tension in the room by the way she shot each of them a glance, then, singing softly to herself, she got busy at the

sink, washing the vegetables and herbs she'd har-
vested from the greenhouse.

"There's a lot to work out, then, isn't there? Look,
I must attend to the rooms now. Maybe we can go for
a hike this afternoon and talk some more? How long
can you stay?" she asked.

"Until tomorrow lunchtime. And can I help you?"

"No, Elsa is here, so she'll help. Also, it would
be against our privacy policy to let you assist me in
guest rooms."

"Fair point. Okay, so one-ish?"

She nodded.

"Good. Thank you for making time for me."

"It's not just for you," she said quietly before ris-
ing from the table and clearing their plates.

"All the same, thank you."

By the time Sunday lunchtime rolled around, they
had spent a good deal of time together—hiking and
talking, yes. But on solving the big question about
how much she'd let him into her life, there'd been
little success. Fletcher shoved his clothes in his pack.
His frustration with the entire situation was doing his
head in. The attraction he'd always felt for Stevie had
deepened into something far more than just physical.
Oh sure, he craved her with every indrawn breath of
his lungs, but he was beginning to understand the
complexities that made her who she was, too.

She'd talked at length about her life here as a child.
With her grandmother and Penny as her guides and
role models. While she'd also opened up a little more

about her marriage, and he felt badly that he hadn't seen past the facade that Harrison had always presented to the unhappiness she'd borne beneath the highly polished surface, she hadn't mentioned her first baby again. Obviously it still hurt Stevie too much to talk about her. It made him all the more determined to show Stevie she could trust him and that she could, hopefully, let him share her load. But even though they'd talked at length about so many things, he was no closer to finding a solution to their problem. She was firm about not leaving Nickerson House but had agreed to him setting up a fund for the baby once it was born—it was money that he felt his child was entitled to, to ensure they would never miss out on any opportunities. It wasn't so bad to want the best of everything for them, was it?

He yanked the zipper closed and hefted the strap onto his shoulder. A final visual check of the room showed he'd left nothing behind. Downstairs, Stevie was at reception, checking out a small group of guests. From the compliments being paid her way, Fletcher had no doubt the group would be back. Stevie's personal touches with the rooms and service made coming here something people wanted to repeat. He knew he did, although probably for entirely different reasons.

Once the others had left, he stepped up to the desk and presented his credit card.

"Oh, Fletcher, you don't need to do that. I asked you to stay."

"I took up the suite. I don't expect you to be out-of-pocket for that," he insisted.

Stevie looked like she was about to argue, but then, with her top teeth firmly embedded in her bottom lip, she took the card and put his payment through before handing him the receipt.

"There. Satisfied?"

"Not even. But could you book the suite for me next weekend, too. We're not done talking, are we?"

She sighed heavily. "No, I guess we're not." She tapped a few keys on the computer. "There, all booked in."

"Thanks. I'd best be on my way."

"I'll come and see you out."

He could smell the delicious fragrance of her hair as she walked past him to open the front door. They walked down the front stairs together. At the bottom, she looked up at him.

"Thanks for coming, Fletcher. And thanks for opening up to me about…before."

He nodded. It hadn't been easy, but it had been necessary. It was one thing he'd learned a long time ago. If you wanted something bad enough, sometimes you needed to face unpleasantness to get it. And he wanted her. Not just her but a life with her, he'd realized as he'd stared at the ceiling of his bedroom for several hours last night.

He stared into her eyes, losing himself in the dark brown irises with their wide black pupils. Eyes that could spit tacks but which, he knew intimately, could be impassioned and clouded with need and desire. He couldn't pinpoint the exact moment he knew he was going to kiss her, but he had no wish to talk himself out of it, either. He lowered his face to hers, felt her warm breath on his face before he leaned in and captured her lips with his own. Her taste was familiar, her response immediate, with her arms coiling around his neck and her mouth moving beneath his as if she were drowning and he was the only way she'd ever breathe again. He recognized the feeling because he felt it himself. Emotion swelled from deep inside him, curling around his heart and squeezing tight, sending fire licking through his veins as every cell in his body focused on the raw connection they shared.

The timing was all wrong. This wasn't how he wanted to leave her, but he knew he had to get on the road, had to resume normality away from the idyll of this weekend with her. Fletcher reached up for her arms and gently lifted them from his shoulders and ended the kiss.

"Think about us, Stevie," he said, his voice sounding rough. "Think about what we could be."

And with that, he got in his car and closed the door, started the engine, and drove away, forcing himself to keep his eyes forward and not to look back.

Twelve

Stevie felt his kiss linger for ages after Fletcher left. It was the kind of kiss that a person tucked away in their memory and savored in quiet moments, over and over again, wondering when they'd next experience such a thing again. She'd lost count of the number of times she'd found herself with her fingertips pressed to her lips, as if she were trying to relive it all over again. But she knew such a thing was futile without the man himself there to deliver it. But he'd be back soon, she reminded herself, and alternately looked forward to it and dreaded it at the same time. He wanted an answer from her.

To distract herself, and in between her normal hotel duties, she spent the next two days with Penny, delving into the pros and cons of running the gourmet-cooking retreats. She was surprised to see how much work Penny had already put into the idea, with budgets and a focus on seasonal produce as well as holiday-themed menus at different times of year.

By Wednesday, they'd agreed on a soft launch and had set up a special social media page to advertise themes, number of spaces and dates available. It had been nerve-wracking blocking out their accommodation for those specific dates, because even a few casual guests could make a difference between a week that broke even or not. But if there was one thing that Stevie had learned, it was she had to commit to something fully to be able to see the kind of results she wanted.

Penny was beside herself with excitement over it all, and Stevie couldn't help but feel buoyed along by her enthusiasm. Perhaps they could make the gourmet sessions work alongside the corporate wellness retreats. After all, good eating and healthy choices were all part of the whole.

Stevie settled herself at her computer and opened her email. There were a few bookings together with correspondence both from her bank and from the company she'd pitched her wellness retreats to. She immediately dealt with the bookings and fired back confirmations and booking reference numbers. Then she took a deep breath and tried to decide which email to open first. The bank's or Maisel Electronics', the potential client. In the end, the Maisel Electronics' email won out.

She slowly counted to three and clicked on the

email, her eyes scanning its contents with an increasing sense of joy. They wanted to come on board in the following year and requested she set up a meeting to discuss the various tiers of services Stevie had proposed. They also advised forwarding her contract to their legal department for their perusal prior to that meeting. Stevie let out a whoop of excitement. This was exactly what she'd been hoping for. It was the first step on the ladder to achieving her business goals. She'd done it. And by herself, too.

She leaped up from her chair and did a little happy dance before heading down the hall to let Penny know the great news. After a celebratory glass of club soda, Stevie returned to her office. It was then she remembered she had yet to open the mail from the bank. She hovered her cursor over the unopened mail for a full thirty seconds before clicking on it. Her eyes scanned the email, looking for the acceptance she'd sought, but it didn't matter how often she did it. The words "we regret that your application has been unsuccessful at this time" did not change.

Every part of her felt as if it had turned to stone. Short of crowd funding, she'd already exhausted every alternative financial avenue to go down. She'd used up most of the money she'd gotten after Harrison's death for the renovations already completed in the main accommodation wing of the hotel and in updating the kitchen. The rest she'd set aside for wages so her staff would not be negatively impacted if occupancy remained unpredictable. What the heck was she going to do now?

The next two days passed in a blur and her nights were no better as she tossed and turned wondering how they were going to keep the retreat contract and still be able to provide the facilities she'd proposed. Of course, she'd put the horse before the cart in soliciting the business before having the finance signed off on, but she'd wanted to show the bank she was being proactive about gearing her business to a higher end of customer than purely the bed-and-breakfast short stays.

Fletcher was due to arrive this evening, she reminded herself. No doubt he'd have suggestions to make—if she were prepared to listen. She tried to tell herself that she wasn't looking forward to seeing him again, but the truth was she'd be lying if she didn't acknowledge that he had never been far from her thoughts this week. Was that why he'd kissed her when he'd left last Sunday? To embed himself into her psyche?

That kiss had been as unplanned as her pregnancy, and yet there had been an inevitability to it, too. The entire time they'd spent together, she'd been unable to push the memory of their lovemaking from her thoughts. Her body had been on high alert, ready for his touch or the least intimation that he remained attracted to her. It was perverse of her to feel that way. She acknowledged that. Especially since it went against every rule she'd set for herself in her new and rebuilt life. But she couldn't argue that he'd been a masterful lover and great company to boot. A friendship like that had a lot to offer. But he wanted more than friendship. He wanted commitment, and she refused to do that.

After bagging all the laundry for the service to collect, she returned to the kitchen just in time to hear the landline for the hotel ring. She grabbed the extension in the kitchen.

"Welcome to Nickerson House, how may I help you?"

"Stevie, it's Fletcher."

Her body warmed to the sound of his voice and she felt her heart rate pick up a little.

"Fletcher, how are you? Are you on the road already?"

"No, that's why I'm calling. Something came up at work and I'm unable to make it this weekend."

"Oh." She meant to say more, but her throat clogged with emotion and her eyes burned with unshed tears.

"Stevie? Are you okay?"

"Sure, I'm fine," she managed before a giant sob escaped from the tension knotted deep in her chest. Tension that had been relentlessly building for the past two days. She swallowed hard. "Sorry about that. It's been tough week. I guess I was looking forward to seeing you more than I thought. But no problem. Just let me know when you can get here next, okay? I gotta go now."

Carefully she hung up the phone, and with tears blinding her vision, she reached for a chair and sank into it before bowing her head in her hands and giving over to the utter helplessness she felt.

* * *

Fletcher looked at his now-blank cell phone screen. She'd been crying. Had something gone seriously wrong? Was it the baby? A cold fist clenched around his heart. Surely she'd have told him if something was that amiss as to upset her so badly. Without thinking, he pressed redial on his phone, and before she could launch into her phone spiel, he spoke.

"Stevie, it's me again. What's wrong? Is the baby okay?"

He heard her breathing shudder at the other end of the call, then she sighed, and all of a sudden, her words came out in tumbled rush.

"It's not the baby. I just got some bad news from the bank. They're not increasing my loan, which puts me in a bad spot because I got that other contract. But without the refinancing, I can't make the necessary changes to the east wing to be able to take on the custom. I don't know what to do."

The utter helplessness in her tone sent a sharp pain scoring through him. She hadn't said it in so many words, but she'd needed him there tonight and he'd let her down.

"Look, leave it with me. I'll come up with something."

"Fletcher, it isn't your problem."

"If it's your problem, then it is my problem. I'll be in touch, okay?"

"Okay."

He hung up the phone and started making calls. The supply debacle had escalated with their second string of options suddenly hiking their prices, then claiming they had prior orders that would take precedence. Added to that, his mom was feeling melancholy about the past and calling him daily. Between the business and his family needing him right now, that didn't leave a lot left over for Stevie and the baby. He'd earmarked having to work through the weekend just to keep all the plates spinning so nothing would come tumbling down. He huffed out a tightly held breath as his obligations here in Norfolk battled with those in Asheville. He came to his decision. Norfolk would have to wait an extra day until he could give it his full attention. In the meantime, he'd have to ask his brother Mathias to step up for him.

By seven o'clock the next morning, he was on Stevie's back doorstep. He could hear her moving around in the kitchen and he rapped on the door.

"Fletcher? My goodness, did you drive all night?"

"I choppered up. I don't have much time, so can we talk?"

"You choppered up? Just to see me? You didn't need—"

"I did," he interrupted. "You were upset."

"Honestly, you didn't have to go to all this bother."

"It was no bother. I used the company helicopter. I've been trying to figure out a solution to your problem and I didn't want to discuss it with you over the phone. But first, can I have a coffee?"

She gestured for him to come in and poured him a coffee from the carafe in the machine and fixed it with cream and sugar, just how he liked it.

"Did you want to sit here or in my office?" she asked, still looking at him as if she couldn't quite believe he was really here.

"I'd prefer our discussion to be totally private, so your office would best."

They went down the hall and he sat opposite her desk. Without preamble, he launched into what he had to say.

"The way I see it, there are three options. All of which are tied into me personally backing your plans for the finalization of Nickerson House into a high-end wellness retreat and spa."

"You, personally? No, Fletcher, that's not necessary. This is my issue and I'll deal with it somehow. There have to be other alternatives that I can explore."

"I'm pretty sure that if the bank that holds your current mortgage and knows you best won't give you a loan, you're pretty much out of options. Anyone else will charge far higher interest rates. I'm prepared to make this simple for you, Stevie, to help you achieve your dream. Option one is that you allow me to buy into Nickerson House as your silent business partner and you use that money for the development. As you've pointed out and as I've seen while staying here, the property has a huge amount of potential to expand into other accommodation opportunities. From an investment point of view, it's a sound choice. Option two is that you accept an interest-free loan from me, repayable in easy installments once the retreat side of business is up and running. This option gives you the freedom to do what you need to without having to worry about starting repayments before you're pulling in a regular income from the retreats."

She'd begun shaking her head the moment he'd made his first suggestion but now she stopped and stared at him defiantly. "What's the third option?"

"That we get married. And you use our money. My dad's death stirred up a lot of things in my life. And Tiffany's leaving me shook up some more. I thought I knew myself, knew what I was doing, but then I had to question everything. And though I know it's not something to be ashamed of these days, the teasing and gossip about us being illegitimate and a false family hurt. I don't want my child to go through that."

Stevie made a sound of distress. "No, Fletcher, whether a child's parents are married or not has no bearing on who they are as a person. It shouldn't define them. Families everywhere are still that, families, whether there has been a legal commitment to one another or not. Marriage isn't the answer. Besides, North Carolina isn't a community-property state and I've already been burned once."

"What do you mean?"

"Most of Harrison's wealth was tied up in his parents' trust, including the roof over my head that I'd mistakenly thought I would have had a right to reside in, even after his death. But since we had no living children, I had a month to clear my things and get out. All I was entitled to was half the value of what we'd accumulated personally since our marriage. Everything else belonged to his parents."

"You're kidding me. They left you high and dry?"

"I assure you I am not kidding," Stevie said in all solemnity. "So you will understand that I don't believe marriage solves everything. Even if I loved someone enough to marry them, I wouldn't. Never again."

She'd been hurt badly, he could see that. Somehow, he had to make her understand that his goal was to help her without strings attached.

"Okay," he said softly. "Marriage is off the table. Which leaves options one and two."

His cell phone beeped discreetly in his pocket, and he took it out to look at the screen. It was his pilot.

"I'm sorry, I have to take this."

"Go right ahead, I'm not going anywhere."

The news wasn't good. A change in the weather had narrowed the window they'd had before they needed to depart for Norfolk. He must get back to the heliport promptly or risk not being able to get home and back to the office as he'd promised his somewhat disgruntled brother.

"Damn, I'm sorry," Fletcher said regretfully as he put his phone back in his pocket and explained the weather situation. "I have to get to the heliport. I'll leave you to think things over. But the sooner you answer me, the faster I can start the process to get you the money."

Stevie stared at him, her mind in turmoil. She was understandably wary of giving Fletcher, or anyone else for that matter, so much control over her. It was something she'd vowed never to repeat. But the man sitting opposite her had not mentioned any strings, and aside from his repeated offer of marriage, the balance of his suggestions could be accepted as good business sense. There was still that niggle of concern lingering in the back of her mind. If she accepted option one, the thought of which made her stomach churn already, would he become as controlling as her late husband was and eventually try to dictate every part of her life to please him?

No, there was no way she could relinquish that much control. Her business, such as it was, was hers 100 percent and always would be until she died or chose to sell it. Which only left option two. She'd be a fool to refuse an interest-free loan, wouldn't she?

"Option two," she blurted. "I'll take option two."

Fletcher's face, already drawn with weariness, changed in an instant.

"I'll get on to the legal side of things first thing Monday. Now, if you'll excuse me, I need to go."

She followed him back to the kitchen, where Penny had reappeared and was busy kneading dough at the counter for her special herbed bread rolls to go with homemade pumpkin soup.

"Smells good, Penny," Fletcher said, sniffing the air appreciatively. "I wish I could stay and try some."

"Going already?"

"Work and weather windows call," he said. He waved as he opened the back door.

Stevie followed him outside, already in a turmoil over the decision she'd made.

"Fletcher, thanks for coming."

"No problem. Try not to worry too much, okay? We'll sort everything out together."

He bent his head and gave her a swift hard kiss and, in the next moment, was striding toward the car he'd obviously hired. He was gone in an instant, and a chilly breeze drove Stevie back indoors.

"That was short and sweet," Penny remarked as she set aside her dough to proof.

"He flew in. I think he expected to stay longer, but bad weather coming in meant he had to leave now."

"Long way to come for a kiss that brief."

Stevie blushed. "He didn't come to kiss me."

Penny dusted off her hands and turned to face Stevie. "No, he didn't, did he? So why was he here?"

Stevie battled with sharing the news with Penny, but the woman had been her sounding board for so many of her problems that it would be stupid to keep her in the dark now.

"The bank refused my application for refinancing to do the improvements for the east wing. Fletcher has agreed to lend me the money."

There, that didn't sound so bad, did it? Why then did she feel as though she were teetering on the edge of a precipice and there would be no end to the fall?

"Wish all our guests were as generous," Penny said with a smirk. "Mind you, he's more than a guest, isn't he? When are you going to tell me the rest?"

"The rest?"

"I'm not a fool, Stevie. You're expecting, aren't you?"

Stevie nodded.

"Have you told him about Chloe?"

"Not about why she died."

"The man deserves to know."

"I know. I just haven't found the right moment. But I will. Soon."

"Good, and I'm glad you've let someone into your heart again. You were never born to be a loner, Stevie."

"Who said anything about my heart being involved?"

Penny sighed. "Well, it's clear as day that he cares for you. If he doesn't, do you think he'd be so quick as to put a whole ton of money at your disposal? Besides, I've seen the way he looks at you. You could do a lot worse, you know. Well, you did, if we're being painfully honest."

"And what if something is wrong with the baby, Penny? It's happened before, and while I know the odds are low, it could happen again. What if he rejects the baby?"

Unspoken, other words echoed in her brain. *What if he rejects me?*

"Then we will deal with it. Honestly, Stevie, he doesn't strike me as being the kind of man who would ignore his responsibilities. Look at how he dropped everything and came to see you this morning. By helicopter, no less. Would your husband have done that? I don't think so."

"They were close friends, Penny. What if underneath it all, he's just the same? He and Harrison were fiercely competitive with one another. What if this is some scheme to one-up a dead man? Pay him back or something?"

"Good heavens, girl! Can you hear yourself? Stop

looking for excuses not to trust him. It's past time to change your thinking. There is nothing of your late husband in Fletcher Richmond. Absolutely nothing. He strikes me as being a good man with a big heart. Don't hurt him, Stevie."

"Don't worry. I don't plan to."

But what about her? What was with the rush of joy she'd felt when she'd seen him? Joy that was rapidly replaced with an urge to reach out and touch him, to feel his strength and to anchor herself to it. That wasn't what she'd spent the last eighteen months retraining herself to do. She was her own anchor. Herself and this house—no one else, especially not Fletcher Richmond.

Thirteen

The flight home had seen them diverted north by about a hundred miles. The diversion forced them to stop and refuel again before they could complete the journey to Norfolk. It was the middle of the afternoon before Fletcher pulled up in the driveway to his house, having given up on heading into the office, and he was surprised to see both Mathias's and Lisa's cars parked on the drive ahead of him. Both had keys to his place, so when he let himself in and heard them talking in the kitchen, he joined them there.

"Oh, so you've arrived back," Lisa said, leaning back against the countertop and crossing her arms.

"As you can see," Fletcher said wearily. "I told Mathias I wouldn't be in until later today."

"That's true. Although, I'm guessing you forgot

you told me you'd be in the office by midday for a meeting with us both before we tackled the supply issue? You didn't answer your phone or your landline here. We came over convinced you'd knocked yourself unconscious or something," said Mathias, opening the fridge to look inside, then closing it again in disgust when he found nothing to nibble on. "Jeez, man, how come you never have any decent food in here and when are you going to get some damn furniture?"

Fletcher closed his eyes and groaned. Guilt slayed him. He'd always put his family first and business second. Today they'd both dropped to dead last and it hurt him to realize that. "I got held up. I'm really sorry to have let you guys down."

"By the woman I saw in the office a couple of weeks ago? The one who walked into your office and said she was pregnant?" Lisa said with a sharp look.

Fletcher held back another groan. His little sister was always far too perceptive for her own good, or his.

"Is she why you have been so mentally absent lately?" Lisa pressed.

"Her name is Stevie, and yes."

There was no point in beating around the bush. They'd know about it all soon enough anyway. He needed coffee. Hell, he needed something way stronger than that.

"Why do you answer Lisa's questions and not mine?" Mathias said with a pained expression.

"Because your questions are dumb," Lisa said with

a poke at his ribs. "I have a box of doughnuts in the car. You want to get them?"

Mathias was gone in an instant. While he got the doughnuts, Lisa started making a fresh brew of coffee. Once Mathias was back, they all settled at the kitchen table.

"Okay, Fletch, give it up. Where were you?" Mathias asked.

"Asheville."

"North Carolina? That's gotta be four hundred miles away."

"Yeah, we struck bad weather coming back and had to divert to another airport."

"Why were you in Asheville?" Lisa said, coming straight to the point.

"She needed me."

Fletcher couldn't help but see the look that passed between his siblings.

"So, let me get this right. You've met a woman, and because she needed you, you took the company chopper and flew there and back and ignored your responsibilities here at work?"

"I knew you two could cope with it. I trained you well." He added that last bit to remind them both he was the eldest.

Lisa tapped a knuckle on the table, drawing Fletcher's attention. "Details, brother. I knew there was something up when she came to the office. She looked anxious. I'm assuming the baby is yours?"

"What? How did I not hear about that?" Mathias asked indignantly. "What happened to our all-for-one-and-one-for-all promise to one another after Dad died?"

"Look, I'm sorry," Fletcher said roughly. "Let me explain."

He summarized going to stay at Nickerson House and meeting up with Stevie again and glossed over the bit where they slept together. "I wasn't expecting to see her again, but when she got confirmation she was pregnant, she came and told me. We've been trying to work through some things."

"Why do I get the impression that's an understatement?" Lisa asked before getting up to pour herself another coffee.

"Stephanie Reed, you say? And now she's Stevie Nickerson?" Mathias asked.

"She was Stevie Nickerson before she met Harrison."

"I vaguely remember meeting her one night when I was out with you, probably about eight years ago. She was a bit of a Stepford wife. I wouldn't have thought she was your type."

Fletcher jumped hotly to Stevie's defense. "She is most definitely not a Stepford wife. I know she was different then, but there were reasons."

"Reasons?"

"It turns out Harrison chose her so he could groom her to be the perfect wife and convinced her to change because she loved him. He took away all her freedom and spirit."

"You're kidding me," Mathias said, a serious expression coming over his face. "There was always an undercurrent about him. I could never understand how you two got to be such buddies. So, is she okay now?"

"Aside from being pregnant, yeah. She's rebuilt her life, reestablished her independence. That's a good thing, I know, but it means she's closed to accepting help or advice from me."

"Advice?" Lisa asked. "Or are you bullying her into what to do?"

Fletcher was affronted. "Bullying? When have I ever bullied anyone?"

"Okay," she conceded. "Perhaps bullying is too strong a word to use. But you do have a habit of rushing in to fix things. We're used to it, and to be honest, we expect it, which was why we were so shocked when you weren't at the office today. We sorted out the supply issue, too, by the way. Seems we are actually capable of our jobs after all."

Lisa smiled to soften her words but her face was all seriousness when she continued. "But back to my point, have you actually asked her what she wants to do?"

"All I know for sure is that she won't agree to a plan for our future as parents. I really want to be a part of my baby's life, guys. And hers. You know what happened to me last time. I won't let that happen again. I deserve a say in my child's life."

"Then, maybe start by listening to her and why she is so reluctant to commit to anything. If her late husband did a number on her mentally and she's recovered from that, then she's a wonderfully strong woman who deserves your admiration and support. It doesn't sound like she needs a knight in shining armor, more a partner. Someone to share the load."

Fletcher was pretty sure that's what he'd offered when he'd asked her to marry him, but then again, as Lisa had so carefully pointed out, he hadn't really stopped to consider how this unexpected pregnancy had derailed the new order of Stevie's world.

"You care about her, don't you?" Lisa probed.

"I've always cared about her," Fletcher admitted. "Ever since the first time I met her, but she was already with Harrison and off-limits."

"What are you going to do about it now?" Mathias asked.

"Figure it out, the way I always do. Thanks, guys. I appreciate you coming here and I really appreciate you taking up the slack at work today. It's time I did some very hard thinking."

Ever since Fletcher's contract had arrived Stevie had been vacillating between signing it or tearing it up. If she chose the latter, she'd have no dependence on Fletcher, which was a very good thing, but if she did that, she would have to delay her business plans and build up the bed-and-breakfast without the spa. Aside from that, she'd still always be connected to him through the baby. She felt so darn conflicted and knew they needed to talk this through.

The paperwork his attorney had sent her had been screened by her lawyer who could see no reason for her not to sign it. It was a simple, interest-free-loan agreement with easy repayments set to commence twenty-four months from date of signing. That was more than ample time for her to have the renovations completed and be making money. And yet, somehow, she couldn't bring herself to sign it. It felt like a betrayal of her promise to herself to rebuild her life and Nickerson House by herself.

This past week, she'd met with builders and decorators, and she had the quotes she needed. All she had to do was sign Fletcher's contract, and everything would come together. It all seemed too simple. And that's why she was pulling up outside Fletcher's house right now. It made sense, if she was going to sign this loan agreement, that she do it with Fletcher, right?

Or maybe you just want to be near him? After all, it's been an entire week since you saw him.

She pushed the thought to the back of her mind and got out of her car, the contract shoved into her large tote. Stevie let herself in through the iron gate at the front of the property and pushed herself to keep going up the short walk to the stairs that led to the front door. The door opened before she could even lift the heavy brass knocker.

He looked tired but still so gorgeous she felt the air get knocked out of her lungs all over again. Why did he have such an immediate effect on her every time she saw him? That curling sensation of warmth began to wind through her body as she met his gaze and saw the steadiness reflected in their gray depths. People said that gray eyes were cold, but they'd never met Fletcher Richmond. There was so much heat in his look she felt as though all it would take to light up would be a single touch.

She forced herself to snap out of it and pasted a smile on her face. "Hi. Thanks for agreeing to see me today."

"I'm glad you could come," Fletcher said warmly. "I was beginning to worry that you'd changed your mind about the loan."

"Not changed my mind, exactly. More that I haven't fully made my mind up just yet."

"Come on in, let's see if I can settle any questions you have."

He sounded so rational, so kind. What the heck was wrong with her? But then again, there was so much about him that reminded her of her late husband. This house, for example, in one of the best areas of Norfolk. At her best guess, it dated from the 1920s, and the interior, what she could see of it as she entered the main hallway, had the beautiful lines and spacious, high-ceilinged rooms that were typical of the era. And the house was huge, even if it did appear to be echoingly empty. It was exactly the kind of opulent space Harrison would have chosen.

"Come through to the kitchen," Fletcher suggested. "We can sit there."

"Have you just moved in?"

"No, I've been here a couple of years. I bought it hoping to make it a family home, like the one I grew up in with my brother and sister. Plenty of space for kids to have their own place but grand rooms to gather in with friends as well. I was engaged when I bought it, but Tiffany took most of the furniture when she broke our engagement. I keep meaning to do something about the place, either furnish it or sell it, but we've been under a great deal of pressure at work, so making a decision here has been on the back burner."

Stevie looked around the kitchen where they had settled at a table. "It seems such a shame not to fill the house with people. I can see why you chose it for your home. It would lend itself well to being a luxury bed-and-breakfast, too. Especially with its proximity to business centers, etcetera. Not everyone is after a cookie-cutter hotel stay. How many bedrooms have you got?"

"Five, all with en suite bathrooms."

"Well, if you ever decide to give up construction, you can always go into business right here," she said with a teasing smile. "So, the loan agreement. I've read it, my lawyer has read it, everything looks very straightforward. I can't help feeling that there must be a catch somewhere."

Fletcher held his hands up as if in surrender. "No catches, I promise. Can we look at it as a friend helping out a friend?"

Her lips pulled into a rueful smile. "I think we kind of bypassed the friend stage, don't you? My lawyer is concerned you aren't charging me interest, for your sake, obviously, not mine."

"Well, that's very kind of them. However, I'm not in this to make money off you. I just want to help. That's all it is. Pure and simple. No strings attached."

"And no coercion, either?" she couldn't help but ask.

He looked affronted. "Coercion? Seriously? You think I'm doing this to make you agree to something else?"

"Well, we are at an impasse about the baby."

"Yes, we are, but that has no bearing on my desire to help you achieve your goals."

How could she be sure of that? Instinct told her she could trust him, but experience showed her that misplaced trust was a dangerous thing.

"Balance the options," he suggested. "On one hand, you have the money you need, interest-free, to make the renovations now so you can expand your business as you had already planned to. On the other, you have to wait until you are in a stronger financial position to borrow more against the house, with interest. Your plans for development and providing a niche product to what is potentially a very lucrative market will be on hold indefinitely. Which one would you rather do? I know which one would appeal to most people with an eye to the future.

"Take a leap, Stevie. Run with the opportunity."

"You're right," she said decisively. "It is a no-brainer."

She reached into her tote and drew out the papers and removed the pen she'd clipped to them earlier. It took only two seconds to turn to the signatory page, and less to scrawl her signature across the line and push the agreement across the table to Fletcher.

"There. It's done."

"Congratulations. You won't regret it."

She looked at her watch and sighed. "I'd better get going. I still need to find a place to stay for tonight."

"Why don't you stay here? You can sleep in my bed. I put fresh sheets on this morning."

"Are you sure? But where will you sleep?"

"On the couch."

"Fletcher, I've seen your living room. You have no couch. Honestly, I'll find a hotel. It isn't high season."

She got up from the table and slung her tote bag over her shoulder. Fletcher stood, too, and placed himself firmly in front of her. To her surprise, he took both her hands in his and looked her square in the eyes.

"Stay…with me."

Butterflies set up a flutter in her stomach. Was he suggesting what she thought he was suggesting? There was a hunger in his gaze, one that she recognized because she felt it herself every time she saw him. It hadn't abated, not even a little, and she'd lost track of the number of times she'd lost herself in daydreams where she'd relived the one night of bliss they'd spent together.

"No strings?" she said with a slight catch in her voice.

His own was far firmer as he replied. "No strings. Just us. Being us."

Again, she hesitated and asked herself if this was something she really wanted to do. She'd sworn off having another relationship, ever, but there was something about Fletcher that drew her on a visceral level. Something that made her heart race and her blood heat when she saw him. Something that made her quell her desire for absolute independence and quietly yearn for more.

No strings? There were always strings but, she reminded herself, they didn't have to trap you. For her, at least, there was only one answer.

"Okay," she said simply.

Fourteen

Fletcher looked at her for a full five seconds, barely able to believe what she'd just said. Then reason kicked in and he reached for her hand.

"Let me show you the room, but first, is there anything you need from your car?"

"I have all my overnight stuff in here," she said, gesturing to her tote bag.

He lifted it off her shoulder. "Here, let me carry that for you."

Then, with her hand still in his, they headed for the stairs. They ascended the wide, curving staircase slowly. He was giving her every chance to change her mind and to back out. In fact, he half expected her to, even as he pushed open the bedroom door and led her into his room. She closed the door behind them and it shut with a very definite click, as if they were shielding themselves from life outside this room and from everything about that life that caused trouble or pain or indecision.

Stevie slipped her feet out of her shoes and walked on the carpeted floor to the windows. She pulled the drapes closed, then turned and looked at him.

"How come you're standing over there?" she asked.

"Just watching you," he said quietly.

He wasn't about to admit that he was imprinting memories of her in his house, in his room, in his mind. He closed the distance between them and reached for her, inviting her into his embrace. As her body settled against his, and her slender arms wrapped around his waist, he felt a sense of rightness in his world. She tipped her face to his, her lips parted in a silent invitation. He didn't need to be asked twice. He kissed her, his lips molding to hers as if they'd been made to be together. When their tongues brushed and met and curled and retreated, it was as if they were doing a dance that transcended time and place.

Fletcher's heart beat so hard against his chest he thought it might leap out, but a gentle touch of a fingertip to the pulse at her neck revealed Stevie was in the same state. He felt her tug at his shirt, pulling it free from the waistband of his trousers, and he hissed in delight as her strong hands stroked his bare skin, sending goose bumps to race over him. The tunic Stevie wore had a zipper at the back, and he eased it down before reaching for the hem of the garment and pulling it over her head. Soon to follow that was the long-sleeved T-shirt and then the matching leggings that hugged her thighs and calves. He took his time undressing her, and she matched him garment for garment, disrobing him until he stood in nothing but his boxer briefs. His erection pressed against the tight fabric and he wanted nothing more than to coax Stevie onto the bed and lose himself inside her beautiful body.

He could see changes in her from the last time he'd seen her naked. Her breasts were slightly fuller and more translucent than before. He traced one bluish vein with a fingertip and relished her sharply indrawn breath as she reacted to his touch.

"You have always been the most beautiful woman I have ever known," he said sincerely, before kissing her again.

She pressed against him, bare skin to skin and it was the most delicious sensation. He ran his fingers down her spine, down to the curve of her buttocks and the backs of her thighs. Her skin was warm and soft, her muscles supple and strong. He hadn't been lying when he'd said she was the most beautiful woman he'd ever known. From the moment he'd first seen her, he'd wanted her with an ache that went soul deep. But she'd been forbidden. Now all he needed to do was to find a way to keep her without clipping her wings.

Her reluctance to commit to another person was understandable, but not everyone was cut from the same cloth. He could only hope that by accepting his offer of a loan, she was opening herself up to him, allowing him into her life, and with any luck, her heart.

Oh, yes, he'd wanted her when he was a younger man, but it was merely the forerunner to how he felt about her now. And while he might not be able to say the words out loud to her, or even admit them to himself just yet, he could show her by word and deed just how much she'd come to mean to him.

They moved to the bed and took their time exploring one another, as if every facet of their bodies was new and exciting all over again. Fletcher savored every moan and sigh as he brought her pleasure. Softly caressing every curve and indentation of her body with gentle fingertips before following each stroke with his lips in a kiss that sealed his silent promise to be there for her.

When he entered her in the fullest affirmation of his unspoken feelings for her, he paused, relishing the feel of her around him, her heat, her strength, the very power of her womanhood. And then he began to move. Stevie's hands reached for him, her hands clutching at his shoulders as if he were her mainstay—her one constant on a stormy sea. And when the waves of their passion broke and lifted her to her ultimate satisfaction, he found his also, his climax sending him over with her.

He cradled her against him in the aftermath, listening to her as their breathing returned to normal, as their hearts slowed and beat in sync. Fletcher reached lazily for the bedcovers and pulled them over their bodies. If they could be this good together, why should they ever be apart again? he thought as he finally drifted off to sleep.

* * *

Stevie woke early and turned to look at Fletcher's face. In sleep, he lost all the tension he carried on his features, the lines on his forehead softening and the tightness around his eyes gone altogether. Her heart twisted, and with the pang came a powerful wave of regret that she'd given in to her own need for him and slept with him again. She ought to have held firm and left when she'd planned to. They'd completed their business. The last thing they'd needed to do was complicate things further by having sex.

She carefully edged her way off the bed and gathered up her clothes and went into the adjoining bathroom to quickly shower and dress. It was still pitch-dark outside and a glance at her watch confirmed it was only 5:00 a.m. She was used to being an early riser, but weariness pulled at her every muscle as she dragged on her clothing from the night before. She picked up her shoes and her tote bag after she reentered the bedroom and silently made her way downstairs through the house. Empty as it was, and with no window treatments, the downstairs was softly lit by the streetlights outside. A far cry from the isolation of Nickerson House, where this time of the morning, the timers would light the public areas to keep guests safe, she thought with a small smile.

Downstairs, she stood in the main foyer and looked around. The house was truly beautiful but lacked personality. How did Fletcher live like this? It was as if he were in a vacuum and his surroundings didn't matter to him at all. He'd mentioned having a tough year and not getting around to decorating the house, but surely he could have at least rented some furniture in the meantime? This was his home, but it had such a feeling of impermanence. Nothing within it reflected the man who lived here. Was this where he expected to have his child visit?

She shook her head as she made her way to the kitchen and poked in the fridge and the cupboards for something quick to eat. If she left soon, she'd be back in Asheville before midday, even allowing for any traffic on the way out of Norfolk. But oddly, she was reluctant to go. And that worried her.

Again, she felt a surge of remorse for the night she'd shared with Fletcher. She'd sent him the wrong message by staying—she knew that now—because there had been an element in his lovemaking that had been far, far more than just sex. Even the words he'd spoken had suggested feelings that had been there for some time, and that frightened her. A sound on the stairs alerted her to his presence. He'd pulled on a pair of pajama pants and a short robe, which he'd left undone, exposing his chest and belly and making her force her eyes away from him before the curl of desire that started in the pit of her belly flamed into something far more demanding and less controllable.

It was exactly the kind of reaction that she wanted to avoid because she knew that her attraction to him would lead her into hot water if she allowed it to take control. She had to remember to keep her distance.

"Good morning. You're up early. Couldn't sleep?" he asked as he flipped the switch on his coffee machine.

"I'm always an early riser," she answered, still not meeting his eyes as she spoke. "Look, Fletcher, there's something I need to say. I'm sorry if staying here last night has sent you the wrong message."

"And just what message do you think I may have incorrectly interpreted?"

"That there can be more between us than what there is already. Nothing has changed as far as I'm concerned. I just want you to be clear on that."

His face hardened, and his eyes narrowed slightly as he looked at her. "Nothing? I beg to differ, Stevie. I have feelings for you. I always have. I tried to be a gentleman about them years ago, but Harrison saw right through me. I think it gave him a sense of satisfaction to know that he had you when I couldn't. But while I may have lusted after you from afar back then, what I feel for you now is far more complicated than that, and far simpler at the same time. There's a deep attraction between us. Don't we owe it to ourselves and our child to explore that?"

"It's nothing. It's just sex."

"Really? Is that what you were thinking last night? It was just sex? No matter how much you might want to deny it, it went way deeper than that. Why lie to yourself when you can have happiness if you'd just let what's happening between us grow? Let your feelings develop into what you deserve to feel. If you just give us a chance together—"

"No. You can be certain that I won't ever consider a longer-term relationship. Our being together has already put me in a position of having another child when I swore I'd never risk that again."

Stevie covered her mouth with her hand, but it was too late, the words were out and Fletcher had heard and interpreted each one exactly as they were meant.

"Stevie, I think you'd better tell me what this is about."

Numbly, she took a seat at the kitchen table. Fletcher moved around behind her to make fresh coffee and shoved a mug in her direction.

"It's decaf. You're okay with that, aren't you?"

She nodded, too wound up to speak but knowing she was going to have to find the strength from somewhere to talk about Chloe. Fletcher sat beside her and angled his chair so he faced her.

"Stevie," he coaxed. "Tell me about your first baby."

"My daughter, Chloe Elizabeth Reed, was born with a chromosomal abnormality called trisomy 18. It causes developmental delays and birth defects that can lead to death within the baby's first year. Chloe was only four weeks old when she took her final breath in my arms." Her voice broke on a sob. It never got any easier to retell the story.

"Stevie, I'm so very sorry. That must have been hell for you both."

"Both? No. You are very much mistaken. When Harrison saw Chloe, he was revolted. He never held her, never helped feed her or change her or bathe her. He'd wanted nothing to do with her from the moment it had been revealed during a scan and subsequent testing that Chloe had the abnormality. Harrison hated imperfection. And he hated the idea that our friends, such as they were, would know we had a less-than-perfect child. No one but his parents knew about the *issue*, as he referred to it. When she was born, he told people there'd been complications with the birth and that we couldn't have visitors. He told me it was our business and ours alone and when she died, he said to me, 'Aren't you glad we didn't tell anyone now? Imagine having to explain *this* to them?'"

Once again, all the bitterness and shock she'd felt at hearing his callous words spread through her like an uncomfortable rash. Fletcher looked at her in shock, a sound of denial coming from him even as she'd spoken. She shook her head.

"You don't think he was capable of that? Then, you didn't know him as well as you thought you did. He'd stopped being the man I'd thought I'd married long before I became pregnant, but I held it together because I'd hoped a child would change things between us and cement our marriage. He thought it would help on the next step of showing he was a dedicated family man. I was so very wrong—the only thing he was dedicated to was the Harrison Reed success train. It took Chloe's death for me to see that.

"The morning of the day Harrison died, I'd told him I was leaving and that I was seeking a divorce. You know what he did? He laughed at me and told me what time he'd be home that evening and to make sure I had dinner on the table on time. We argued viciously before he left. I was already driving home to Asheville when I got a call from his father's personal assistant to say he'd been killed. Harrison's father couldn't even bring himself to tell me the news himself. I stayed for the funeral but the day after that I walked away with nothing but Chloe's ashes, the clothes I was wearing and the photo album recording Chloe's short life. And I promised myself and my dead baby that I'd never go down that road again. *Never.*"

Fifteen

Fletcher sat there in absolute shock. No wonder Stevie was so adamant about not getting together. She was clearly still suffering some form of post-traumatic stress. But through the shock, anger began to form. A dark, seething anger toward his late friend. How could Harrison have been that kind of person? Who in their right mind thought it was right to treat others that way, and when had he changed so very much? The more he thought about it, the more he realized he'd been equally fooled by the man he'd considered his best friend in college, and that made him mad at both Harrison and himself for not seeing through the facade so cleverly painted.

That Stevie wasn't more damaged from her relationship with a man who had vowed before friends and family to love and honor her and then done anything but that, was a blessing. But she was damaged, and he needed to show consideration for that. And, considering how her last pregnancy had ended, he fully understood her wish not to have another child. But she was pregnant, because of him. He wanted to help her, and being able to show her how important that was to him to do that for her, was nigh on impossible. Her heart had become an impenetrable fortress. He could only hope that with a whole lot of care and steadiness over time that she'd begin to see that he was being honest and true with her.

But it had to be her choice, he accepted that now. He couldn't coerce her or trick her into what he wanted because that would make him no different than Harrison, and if there was anything of which he was now certain, it was that he was nothing like his old friend.

He cleared his throat of the emotional knot that had lodged there. "Stevie, I will support you and the baby no matter what. And if you'll let me, I will make certain that you have the best doctors and specialists all the way through this pregnancy so we can put your mind at ease and cope with whatever comes our way."

"Look, Fletcher, don't get me wrong. I am grateful for everything you've offered. But it doesn't change my mind on us. I'm sorry if what we shared last night led you to think otherwise."

"No, I'm pretty sure I'm clear on your thoughts on that subject."

"Good. Well, I'd better head back home. Tonight

we have a small bus tour arriving for a two-day stay. I need to be certain we have everything in hand before they check in."

"I understand. Let me walk you to your car."

Outside the air was cold and damp, and Fletcher's feet froze on the wet concrete of the sidewalk. He opened Stevie's car door for her and held it as she settled behind the wheel.

"Travel safe, okay? Let me know when you're home."

"Okay, but you don't have to worry about me. I'll be fine."

Worrying about her was becoming a life habit, he realized. "Humor me, please?"

She rolled her eyes. "Sure, fine. Now, are you going to let that door go and head back inside before you begin to resemble an ice cube?"

He cracked a smile, but inside he felt as if he was losing his grip on something very important to him, and by her leaving, it lessened his chances of ever holding on to it again.

"Just one last thing," he said before bending down.

He tipped up her chin and he kissed her, pouring all his feelings into the embrace as much as he was able, given the cramped circumstances. To his relief, she didn't pull back and didn't push him away. In fact, when he finally straightened, closed her door and watched her drive away, he wondered if she hadn't found the kiss as bittersweet as he had.

Stevie's 4x4 ate up the miles toward Asheville. Thankfully, there were no incidents on the road to slow her journey and aside from a couple of toilet breaks, she didn't waste time anywhere. All the way home, her mind kept turning over the conversation she and Fletcher had shared this morning. The younger her, the one who'd been swept off her feet by Harrison Reed, would have leaped to accept what Fletcher was offering. But that wide-eyed, naive girl didn't exist anymore. In her place was a woman who bore hurts that went soul deep. Hurts she had no desire to compound by repeating past mistakes.

And the closer she got to Nickerson House, the more she realized that it was her home base, her security, her sanctuary. And she was good with that. Come what may, she never wanted to do anything that might jeopardize this home that had been in her family for generations. Yes, it was a responsibility, but one she gladly took on because it was hers—all hers. When she pulled into the driveway, a sense of rightness and belonging filled her, and she patted her lower belly gently.

"We're home, baby. Safe home."

As she'd promised, she duly sent a text to Fletcher to let him know she had arrived. He sent back a thumbs up, which made her smile. She'd found leaving him this morning far more difficult than she'd imagined it would be, and that wasn't necessarily a good thing.

Penny had come out the back door as Stevie pulled up.

"Good to see you back. Any interesting takeaways from the hotel you used last night?"

"I, uh, I didn't stay at a hotel."

Penny came to a sudden halt. "Dare I hazard a guess as to where you stayed?"

Stevie refused to make eye contact. "I have no doubt you would be correct."

"Does this mean you two are an item?"

"Absolutely not."

"No good in the sack then, huh?"

"Penny!"

"Well, you can't blame me for asking. Sometimes the window dressing can be deceptive, and his window dressing is pretty darn good, don't you think?" Penny pushed with a smile on her face.

"We spoke about the loan and it was late. Fletcher kindly offered me his bed. There's nothing further to discuss."

Stevie's voice was sharp and clipped, and it had the desired effect on Penny's nosiness.

"Well, I'm sorry to hear that. He seems a nice guy."

"Can we drop the subject now, please? You know how I feel about it. Remind me again what time the bus tour is due to arrive."

Penny gave her the details. "The rooms are aired and made up with fresh toiletries in the bathrooms. No doubt you'll want to do a final inspection, but there's nothing else you need to do."

"And the special meal for tonight is all in hand? Or do you need my help in the kitchen?"

"Nope, Elsa and I have it all under control. I've booked a couple of girls from town to wait the table."

"Great, thanks. I'll go double-check the rooms, and then I'll be in my office if you need me."

Penny nodded and carried on to the vegetable garden. Stevie watched her go. She knew the older woman was only looking out for her and wanted her to have the kind of relationship Penny herself had with Cliff. But she certainly knew how to overstep Stevie's boundaries on the subject. She went up the back stairs and into the kitchen, where she inhaled a hint of the delicious aromas of the food being prepared for the special dinner they were providing the tour group. While essentially they were solely a bed-and-breakfast, it was good business to extend to an evening meal for special occasions. Stevie had high hopes for more referral business coming through from this group of retirees and their tour company.

She dropped her tote bag in her room upstairs and went through to the guest wing and was well satisfied with what she found. The new range of handcrafted eco-friendly toiletries they provided were proving popular with guests, and Stevie had begun a side-line of full-size products for guests to purchase if they wanted them. The manufacturer, a small outfit in town, was only too happy to keep up the supply. It was all part of the symbiotic relationship Stevie had worked so hard to build with locals since she'd taken over Nickerson House, and it gave her immense satisfaction to know that her hard work was all paying off. And, while she couldn't have done it without the help of her incredibly supportive staff, when it came

down to it, these were her ideas coming to fruition—
her success.

It made her think hard about the expansion plans
she had. Was she hoping for too much too soon? Was
she overreaching her boundaries? Sure, if the pandemic hadn't caused such a massive change in people's habits when it came to travel, she'd have been
able to do this on her own or at least been in a better position with the bank to get the additional funds
she needed. But if she thought long and hard about
things, what was so bad about where she was now?
And with a baby on the way, could she even give the
attention she needed to additional development and
managing a larger team of staff?

She was still mulling this over when she got ready
for bed that night. She checked her phone before turning off her bedside light. No messages, not even one
from Fletcher. Why was she even expecting one from
him? She'd made things clear on where she stood
before leaving Norfolk this morning. But it didn't
stop her thinking about last night, or the way they'd
joined together as seamlessly as two halves of one
whole. Was she doing the right thing keeping him at
arm's length now? Logic and the scarred woman inside her told her yes, but there was a little voice at the
back of her mind that challenged her and urged her
to rethink her stance. At some stage she'd have to let
him into her life, for the baby, but she didn't want to
think about that now. She didn't want to think about
anything. She pushed the challenge away with some

effort, and turned off the light and settled into her large, lonely bed.

By morning, she'd worried herself into a knot of tension. A knot she knew would only be loosened if she took drastic steps. She was edgy as she shared breakfast with Penny in the kitchen.

"Bad night?" Penny asked as she poured Stevie a second mug of tea.

"I had a lot of thinking to do. I've decided not to accept the loan from Fletcher and not to undertake the expansion at this time."

There, she'd said it out loud. Now to wait for the fallout.

"I see," Penny said heavily and eased onto her chair at the table. "You've obviously given this a great deal of thought, considering those dark circles under your eyes. It can't have been easy to reach your decision. I know how much you wanted this."

"Thank you for not judging me on this, Penny," Stevie said quietly. Telling Penny had been one of her greatest fears. She'd been so supportive of the idea every step of the way. "I still want the expansion, but when I do it, it'll be on my own terms. I don't want to be beholden to anyone."

Penny nodded. "I can understand that. And Maisel Electronics, what will you tell them?"

"The truth, I guess. That due to circumstances out of my control, I am not in a position to fill their requirements just now. And keep my fingers crossed it doesn't bounce back with bad publicity for us going forward."

"And Fletcher? Have you told him?"

"Not yet, but he will be told. And I think, for now, it would be best not to see him again for a while."

At least, not until she got her act together when it came to her feelings for him. Leaving him yesterday had been so much harder than she'd anticipated, and that left her utterly confused. She should be able to turn this emotional behavior off like a tap. Maybe it was just pregnancy hormones or something, but she couldn't keep her mind completely clear of him at any hour of the day, least of all when she was tossing and turning in her sheets at night.

Stevie followed up with her lawyer, asking him to send an urgent letter to Fletcher saying she was withdrawing from the loan agreement. It made sense, she kept telling herself. If she wasn't prepared to enter an emotional relationship with him, then she shouldn't be standing there with her hand out to accept his money, either, and this way she could minimize contact with him to be solely with regard to the baby.

That done, she settled in to prepare to welcome the hotel's new guests.

The following day she was congratulating herself with how smoothly things had gone with Maisel Electronics. They were disappointed, of course, but handled her withdrawal from the proposal with a smooth professionalism that gave her hope for the future. When the hotel phone rang, she absently picked up without checking the caller ID.

"Welcome to Nickerson House," she said in her hotel-proprietress voice.

Fletcher's voice filled her ear. "What are you doing, Stevie? I made the offer of that loan in good faith. Why are you withdrawing from it?"

"I did some hard thinking, Fletcher, and to be honest, I decided it wasn't fair to you to accept the money," she said carefully.

"I don't get it, Stevie. There were no strings attached, no obligations but to start repayments in two years' time. What changed?"

Trust him to get straight to the point. Stevie sighed and took a moment to get her thoughts clear in her head—not an easy prospect when she was talking to Fletcher. And wasn't that more than half the reason why she'd chosen to withdraw from him completely? If she truly let him into her life, all the way, wouldn't she lose herself—all her hard-won strength and independence—too?

"Look, Fletcher, the other night made things clear for me. It's me. I can't see you and not want to be with you."

There, she'd admitted it.

"Tell me why that's a bad thing," he coaxed.

The tone of his voice was rich with a need to understand and she found it difficult to keep her defenses up against him. From anyone else she would suspect this level of compassion to be a front, just a stopgap until the person got what they really wanted, and if she was 100 percent honest with herself, maybe there was a small part of her that remained wary. But Fletcher deserved to know the truth. All of it.

"It's a bad thing because I can't trust myself not to

fall head over heels in love with you, to the exclusion of everything else in my life. I've worked too hard to allow that to happen again."

"Let me get this right. Even after getting to know me, you still think I'm like Harrison?"

He sounded angry, but not in a highly emotional sense, more a profound, simmering anger and disapproval, which made his voice sound deeper and harder than before. Instinctively she felt everything inside her shrink. She hated confrontation and had schooled herself long ago to do whatever it took to avoid it. But, she reminded herself, she wasn't that person anymore. She was stronger now. She had a mind and a voice of her own, and she wasn't afraid to defend them.

"Look, I'm sorry. I don't trust myself. And, yes, if I'm totally honest with you, Fletcher, there's a part of me that still doesn't trust you, either. I apologize if that is painful to you, but it's just the way it is. I decided it wasn't fair to you to accept your financial assistance, without being prepared to accept you, too."

"And you don't think I deserved to be a part of that decision, Stevie? You say you're sorry, but you're not even giving us a chance."

"Like I said, I'm too afraid to do that. I will not be dependent on any man. I'm finally where I want to be in my life. Where I always saw myself back when I was a teenager with a dream for Nickerson House. I don't need a man to make my life complete, and I don't need his money, either."

"And what of your development plans? How are

you going to cope without the expansion, without the revenue from the contract you were on the verge of signing?" he demanded.

"The expansion is on hold. I know I'll cope, Nickerson House will cope, without the additional business at this time. I'll work on increasing occupancy with what I already have to offer. I'm just not prepared to give up my hard-fought-for independence. Not when I've finally learned to put myself first.

"Fletcher, don't worry about the baby. You will always have reasonable access. We will work something out that is fair, I promise. I will send you updates on the pregnancy, but for now it's goodbye."

Sixteen

The day after their conversation, Fletcher was still left stunned. He'd thought they'd been making headway, that Stevie had begun to lower her guard and let him into her heart. Making love with her had meant everything to him. Had it honestly meant so little to her? He understood trust was a major issue with Stevie, that's why he'd offered the no-strings-loan agreement. It was his greatest wish to see her achieve her dreams for Nickerson House, and making the money available to her as an interest-free loan seemed to be the best way he could do that. But she'd walked away from that dream, too.

He respected her wishes, despite everything in him fighting against the logic of it, and his heart urged him to go and see her. Hadn't she admitted to him that seeing him made her want to be with him? But then, wouldn't that be using her own emotions against her? Wouldn't that make him as bad as Harrison had been? Fletcher clenched his fists in frustration. If the man were still alive, Fletcher would be hard-pressed not to strangle him right now. He smiled cynically. And wasn't that ironic? Because if Harrison were still alive, then Stevie would possibly still be with him. Even though she'd planned to leave him, Fletcher doubted Harrison would have let her go easily.

He expelled a frustrated burst of air from his lungs. He needed to hit the gym. Pound out some miles on a treadmill, then do the same on a punching bag and work out this tension that bound him in chains.

"Problem?" Mathias asked from the door to Fletcher's office.

Fletcher started. He'd been so locked in his thoughts he hadn't even heard Mathias come in and close the door behind him. His brother sat and stared at him, concern very clear on his face.

"Fletch, we need to talk. Luckily for you, I drew the short straw, so I'm going to keep this short and sweet. You missed the online meeting with Logan and Keaton in Seattle yesterday afternoon. I don't need to know your reasons or why you didn't see fit to put in your apologies, but you seriously need to get your head back in the game, because the way you are now, it's impacting everyone here at Richmond Construction, one way or another."

"I know, I haven't been pulling my weight. I'm sorry," Fletcher apologized. "I think I've finally realized I can't be all things to everyone. This isn't the kind of job anyone can do in half measures and that's all you've been getting from me. Things are precarious enough as it is. No one can afford to drop the ball right now, especially not me."

Fletcher hated that it had come to this. That the situation with Stevie was impacting everything that was important to him. But how important was it really? Was his work here his reason for being, the way he'd always thought it was?

A clear realization bloomed in his mind. Since his father's death, Fletcher had been so busy putting out metaphorical fires left, right and center that somewhere along the line his heart had ceased to be engaged in what he was doing. Everything had become a chore to be dreaded rather than a challenge to be relished. The truth echoed in his mind. Richmond Construction wasn't his dream. His dream, his heart's desire was tied up in family and not in the pursuit of unending wealth.

Matthias cleared his throat. "Fletch, it's not all your fault. We haven't exactly picked up the slack unless we had to. You've kept doing your work and Dad's. We need to come to a better sharing of responsibilities."

"I think it's more than that. I've lost my love for what I do here. The cut and thrust of winning another contract or seeing a job to completion is gone."

"You're not talking about quitting, are you?"

Fletcher nodded. "I don't know, entirely. It was

different when Dad was alive, before all the crap hit the fan. But my heart honestly isn't in it anymore."

"Tell me you just need a break. We can work around it. Lisa and I will work with the team to—"

"Mathias, no. Look I wish I'd recognized sooner that I haven't been offering my best for some time, but my heart just isn't in it. I think I need to move on, for all our sakes."

"It's this business with Stevie Nickerson, isn't it?" Mathias said with some sympathy.

"Part of it is, yes. I'd be lying if I said any different. But it's not just that. Even before I went away last December, I was unsettled. Three months later, I still feel the same way."

"What can Lisa and I do to help?" Mathias said.

"I need to take a few steps back. Really evaluate what I bring to the organization and to you all and if someone else could do it better. I think, you're right, doing the work of two people has taken a toll and destroyed any work/life balance I might have had, but that's not the only reason I feel this way. Let's look to creating another role within the company, maybe even two—high level executives that can take up the slack and at the same time bring fresh blood and ideas to what we're doing. We've all been stressed out here, what with Dad and the pandemic, nothing is the same for any of us. Let's work on some kind of transition to restructuring. I don't expect to walk out the door tonight and never come back, but I'd like to think that in the next few months, the company will be in a position to let me go."

Mathias sighed. "I can't say I'm happy about this. Not being able to bounce ideas off you whenever I feel like it isn't something I'm looking forward to."

"It's going to be a big change for all of us. But you know I'll always be there for you if you need me. And I'll remain a shareholder, so you'll have to account to me one way or another," Fletcher added with a teasing laugh.

"Are you going to stay in town and try something new, or are you going to Asheville?" his brother asked.

"For now, I'll stay in Norfolk. However my kid is going to be growing up in Asheville. Ideally, that's where I need to be in the future, that said, I don't want to crowd Stevie or make her feel like I'm intruding on her world. It's something I need to work on because if I don't get this right, I won't get to be a regular part of my kid's life."

"You're a braver man than I am," Mathias commented.

"Actually, I'm not. I just know I have to do this, because I don't want to spend the rest of my days regretting it if I don't."

For the next several weeks, Fletcher was tied up in meetings with Lisa and Mathias and various department heads at Richmond Construction as well as attending a very challenging meeting with the board. He'd been aiming for a four-week period to lead up to easing his working ties with the company. In the end, it took six. They'd promoted one existing staff member and hired on another while Lisa and Mathias had also restructured their roles. Overall, the future looked bright for Richmond Construction going forward and Fletcher would remain in a consultancy role.

Having had time to think about things a bit more, Fletcher realized that problem solving was the one thing that gave him the most satisfaction and without the personal involvement with the company that he'd had before, he started to think about a role as a business consultant, moving forward. It was something he could do from anywhere and the constant change in environments would still keep him fresh at the same time.

Their mom, Eleanor, had railed at him over the phone for what she saw as ditching his responsibilities to the family. However, she'd quieted when Fletcher had told her about the baby and had eventually, reluctantly given her blessing.

Through all the changes he was undertaking including, finally, furnishing his house, Stevie was never far from his thoughts. The urge to call her or see her never left him, but he was determined to respect her space, always mindful of the adage that if you loved something you needed to let it go. If it came back to you, it was yours, but if it didn't it never was yours to begin with.

He sat on his new couch in the main sitting room of his house and stared at the empty fireplace in front of him. It reminded him of sitting with her on Christmas night and simply enjoying her company. Love? It was a complicated concept at the best of times.

He thought he'd loved Tiffany, had planned a life together with her, but his past affection for his ex was nothing on his attachment to a particularly stubborn woman in Asheville.

He turned the idea over and over in his mind, allowing the feelings he had for Stevie to fill him, instead of pushing them away in frustration. Yes, she was obstinate, but she also was loyal to her core and cared about her people whether they be staff or guests at her hotel. Sure, she was inflexible on accepting help, but equally she was resourceful and determined and single minded about creating her own success. And when it came to making love?

Fletcher groaned in frustration. This was torture. But as hard as it was, he had to admit to himself, if no one else, that he had fallen in love with Stevie Nickerson. He wanted to shelter her and protect her but he wanted her to grow from strength to strength and achieve her goals at the same time. She was the first thing on his mind each morning and the last thing in his thoughts at bedtime. He wished she would allow him to help her, but he knew that she wouldn't be who she was if she didn't fulfil her plans herself. In time, maybe she'd grow to see that she could have the best of both worlds, being independent but learning to accept help where needed. And he'd have to wait until that day came and he needed to be ready for it, too.

He'd been playing with ideas about how she could achieve her goals with the wellness spa and retreat. There were other options. Not specifically what she'd wanted to offer, but maybe a gateway to get her to that point. It would mean liaising with other businesses in town, providing a combined service with the spa facilities at a local clinic and her own existing accommodation. It would force her to keep numbers small for now, but allowed room for expansion once her cashflow improved and it would have the added benefit of boosting a local day spa clinic as well, or even a rotation of clinics.

He itched to call her and discuss it with her, but felt that perhaps an email with a proper business proposal laid out might be a more astute way to reach out. Would she still consider it an intrusion? He could only wait and find out. But first, he needed to do his research and see whether the idea was feasible.

He was kept busy over the next couple of days. Word had gotten out about his business consultancy and he had appointments lined up in his diary that would keep him very busy if each potential client went ahead. It was heartening to see he had chosen well when he'd set his feet on this path, and for the first time in a very long while he was excited about the future.

Fletcher was strict about his working hours. Sure, he was setting up something new but he also understood he needed a better balance in his life, which meant leaving work in his office and closing the door behind him by the end of every day. Working from home had its distinct advantages but he could already see that as his consultancy took off he would need a couple of support staff. Whether they worked with him in rented office space or whether they worked remotely, as virtual assistants, he was uncertain just yet.

In the meantime, he noted the date on his calendar and remembered that Stevie would be around eighteen weeks pregnant by now. He'd bought a pregnancy book so he could understand better how their baby was progressing. The whole process fascinated him, and he had nothing but the utmost respect for Stevie and what her body was going through. Had she had the tests yet to find out whether their child had trisomy 18? He knew it was an overwhelming fear for her, and it had become a constant worry in the back of his mind, too. Equally, he had to trust she would communicate with him about the baby sometime soon.

As if he'd conjured her up by thought, Stevie's name lit up on the face of his phone with a message. He opened it and was confused for a minute, until he realized he was staring at an ultrasound still of the baby. The picture was blurry and some of it indistinct, but he could clearly make out a head and the baby's spine. *His* baby's head and spine, he realized with an overwhelming surge of emotion.

He texted her straight back. Thank you. That means a lot to me.

He waited a few minutes, wondering if she'd answer him and had all but given up when his phone began to ring. He answered the call and forced himself to sound relaxed.

"Thanks for the picture," he said on answering. "Is everything okay?"

"I hope so. I've been tested, you know, for the baby having trisomy 18?"

"I was reading about that. I understand they can gauge your risk through using your age, results of a blood test and ultrasound?"

"Yes, that's right—it's not definitive, but as you said, it can be an indicator as to level of risk. I had the test and ultrasound done last week."

Last week? And she only sent him the picture now? While he felt a deep pang of disappointment that she hadn't invited him to come with her for the ultrasound, she had sent him a photo, even if it was seven days later.

Fletcher swallowed to clear the lump that had risen in his throat. "So that's our kid, huh? I don't know much about babies, especially this little, but everything looks great to me."

She laughed on the other end of the phone, and Fletcher felt his lips pull into an answering smile.

"Have you got your test results?" he asked.

"That's why I'm calling you. The doctor has asked me to come in to the clinic tomorrow to discuss them and I... Look, I know it's short notice, but I don't want to go alone. Especially if it's going to be bad news. I know I could ask Penny, but you're the baby's father and I'd like you to be there too."

She sounded scared now she'd come to the point of her call and he could completely understand it.

"Tell me what time and where. I'll be there for you," he said without hesitation. "Unless you'd rather I drove you."

He didn't bother to add the words, *in case it's bad news*. But if it was, there was no way she'd be in any reasonable condition to drive herself.

"Could you come and get me? The appointment is at three in town."

"I'll make sure I'm there at two-thirty so we have plenty of time to find parking."

"Thank you, Fletcher. I really appreciate you coming with me."

He closed his eyes, feeling slightly guilty that he could savor the fact that she needed him, especially given exactly why.

"No problem. I'm here for you, Stevie. Always. You can rely on that."

As they ended the call, he could only hope that she understood the promise that had remained unsaid. *You can rely on me.*

Seventeen

Stevie perched on the edge of her seat while Fletcher sprawled in his as if he had no worries in the world. She knew his relaxed demeanor was a front. She'd gotten to know him well enough to see the tells when he was tense—the slightly drawn brows, the ever-so-tightly clenched jaw—even though he might not be showing it with his body language. She thought back to the last time she was pregnant when she received the confirmation alone. Even then Harrison hadn't been engaged with the baby and right now it struck her that as much as she'd tried to believe otherwise, to protect her own battered heart, Fletcher was not at all like her late husband. She hadn't realized until now that asking Fletcher to come with her today had been a test of sorts. One he'd passed with flying colors. He'd said he'd be here for her and he was.

Not only that, but she'd asked for space, and he'd given it to her. No pressure, no demands, but there for her immediately when she needed him. Was that why it felt so right to be sitting here with him now? Last week, when she'd gone for the ultrasound, she'd felt guilty for not including Fletcher. Oh, sure, she'd rationalized that he'd be busy and unable to come, but the second she'd put out a call for him he had dropped everything for her and was here right now. That had to count for something, didn't it?

Dr. Martin leaned forward with a smile on his face.

"Stevie, I'm very happy to tell you that the preliminary results from your blood tests and your ultrasound show that your baby is at very low risk for trisomy 18. In fact, the fetus looks strong and healthy. Of course we can continue with quad screening in another month or so, but for now, I'd like to prescribe that you sit back, relax and enjoy your pregnancy."

Tears stung Stevie's eyes and began to roll down her cheeks. Dr. Martin pushed a box of tissues toward her and she grabbed a handful to absorb her tears and to blow her nose.

"Thank you, Doctor," she said.

Relief coursed through her. Of course, she knew she wasn't entirely out of the woods, but to be considered low-risk was everything she'd hoped for. There would be more testing later in the pregnancy, for her own peace of mind if nothing else. And, to help her prepare should there be problems of any kind. But for now, she knew she could let herself fall in love with her baby—something she'd been so frightened to do up until this moment.

Stevie turned to Fletcher and grabbed his hand. "Isn't that great news?" she asked him.

"The best," he said, lifting her hand to his lips to kiss her knuckles.

They took their leave of the doctor and headed out. When they reached Fletcher's car, he wrapped her in his arms and held her. His silent strength soothed the last of the frayed edges inside her in ways that she'd never expected. This was what it was like to share a responsibility with someone. This was what it was like to have unquestioning support. She hugged him back, reluctant to let go now they were in physical contact.

A car passing by hooted its horn and against her ear, she heard Fletcher's low chuckle.

"I'm so glad you were with me," Stevie said, reluctantly pulling free and looking up at him. "I don't know how I would have coped if it had been bad news."

"You're strong. You would have coped. But never alone. You'd have me and Penny and no end of support. And when you're ready, my family, too. Lisa can't wait to be an aunt and my mom a grandmother. Even Mathias has admitted to buying a teddy that he said he couldn't resist. Mathias!" Fletcher laughed out loud.

She felt all teary again at his words. The fact his family were also wanting to support her and be a part of her child's life was far more than she'd ever anticipated. It was all a little overwhelming. "Thank you," she whispered before she started to cry again.

Fletcher didn't hesitate. He pulled her back into his arms and stroked her hair, soothing her until she calmed down again.

"I think we should celebrate," he suggested. "Shall we have dinner together tonight?"

"Sure, I think that's a great idea."

Fletcher let her go and opened the car door so she could get in. "Do you have a favorite restaurant? My treat."

She waited for him to settle behind the steering wheel before she answered. "You know, I don't feel like being among strangers. Do you mind if we eat at the house? I can make us something special."

Fletcher smiled at her, and she felt the warmth of it all the way through to her bones. It thawed the tension that she'd been living with since she'd severed contact with him and lit an ember of need in her that almost took her breath away with its ferocity.

"That would be great. Now, how about I get you home."

She drew in a sharp breath as a thought occurred to her. "I'm sorry Fletcher, I didn't even think to offer you a room at Nickerson House. Do you—"

"It's okay, I've booked a room here in town. What time should I come over?"

"How does six thirty sound?"

"I'll be there. What can I bring?"

"Just yourself," she smiled and realized how much she was truly looking forward to this.

When Penny heard what Stevie had planned, she helped where she could and made certain that she was scarce by six o'clock. They had decided to serve dinner in the kitchen. The main dining room of the house was too formal and way too big, and the old breakfast parlor was not yet fit for company.

Stevie checked her reflection in the mirror. She'd been undecided for far too long about whether to wear her hair up or loose and, in the end, had gone for something halfway in between. The messy bun with plenty of hair loose around the edges made her feel like an old-time heroine, and the loose, below-knee dress she'd chosen to wear tonight fit with the hairstyle perfectly. She rested her hand on her belly as she checked her appearance in the mirror. There was barely a bump there, but she felt a powerful connection to this child, conceived as a consequence of her and Fletcher's first night together.

The reassurance her doctor had given her this morning had made everything about the rest of the day appear lighter and brighter. And now she and Fletcher got to celebrate that news tonight. She hadn't been able to stop thinking about him since he'd dropped her back to the hotel. It wasn't just the strength of his presence, or the scent of his cologne that always did things to her equilibrium, it was the solid confidence he had about him. There was no artifice, no coercion—just simply, him. Since she'd turned down his loan and ceased contact, she'd missed him more than she'd wanted to admit and she'd been forced to confront her fears with a painful honesty.

She turned away from the mirror and pushed her thoughts away, the way she always did. But deep down she knew she was delaying the inevitable. She just needed the courage to take the leap. To trust. To care. And maybe, to love. Was she brave enough?

She made her way downstairs just as Fletcher let himself in through the front door. He stopped and looked up at her, and the expression on his face was both raw and beautiful at the same time. She smiled and traveled the last few stairs to stand in front of him.

"Welcome to Nickerson House," she said with a smile teasing around her lips.

"Thank you. These are for you." He handed her a stunning bouquet of spring blooms in delightfully bright colors.

"Oh, Fletcher, you didn't need to," she protested.

"Yes, I did. And these are for you, too." He presented her with a box of her favorite candies from the specialty store in town, together with a bottle of wine. "It's nonalcoholic, so we can both toast to our kid's future."

He'd gone to a lot of effort for her, she realized with a flood of gratitude.

"Thank you so much. Come on through to the kitchen. I hope you don't mind us eating in there. I just felt it was cozier and more familiar to us both."

"No problem at all. It's one of my favorite rooms in the house."

In the kitchen, he got two wine glasses from the large, old glass-fronted dresser and opened the wine. Stevie moved around the kitchen, acutely conscious of him being in here with her. He'd removed his jacket and hung it over the back of a chair, and beneath it, he wore a fine sweater—cashmere by the look of it. It fit him perfectly and sculpted his body as though it was a second skin, reminding her all too vividly of what it had felt like to skim her palms over those muscles and feel the warm, vital strength of him beneath her hands.

A sharp pull of need shot through her body, and she forced herself to pay attention to the food she was checking. Now wasn't the time to be thinking about what it had been like to make love with him, and yet she couldn't shift the memories from her mind no matter what she did.

They indulged in small talk as she set their appetizers on the table and invited him to sit. Mostly her asking him questions about where he was living and what he was doing to fill his days. By the time they'd moved on to the main course, a mustard chicken casserole she'd put together and served with boiled baby potatoes, garnished with butter and chopped parsley, and freshly steamed broccolini, she was done with idle chatter.

She deliberately laid down her knife and fork and stared at him across the table. Obviously sensing her direct gaze, he looked up and mirrored her actions.

"What is it, Stevie? Are you okay? I know it can't be the food that's bothering you because everything has been amazing. I had no idea you were such a great cook on top of everything else."

"I'm fine, and thank you for the compliment. I guess I wanted to apologize for dragging you away from work at such short notice. Having you there with me today was an incredible support. Please know how grateful I am."

Ugh, and as if that didn't sound stilted and weird, she thought. She watched as he lifted his glass and took a sip of the wine and swallowed it before putting the glass back down.

"The way I see it, it's simple, to be honest. I'm here because you needed me and I'll always be here for you when you need me. By the same token, I honestly want to respect your space. I would like to think that maybe we can find some middle ground in the near future that will continue to make things easier on you and that would allow me to be there for both you and the baby."

"But what about your work? You can't just keep dropping everything and rushing here at a moment's notice."

"If that's what it takes, that's what I'm prepared to do."

"I can't see Lisa and your brother—Mathias, right?—being too thrilled with that."

"It won't bother them. I've stepped away from Richmond Construction."

"What? Because of me?" she said, shocked.

He sighed and folded his napkin, placing it neatly next to his plate. "Partly because of you, sure, but mostly because of me. I haven't been happy or satisfied with my work in a very long time and I finally decided to do something about it. I still consult with Richmond Construction, but I've found a new career path. One that I actually look forward to each morning when I wake up."

"Tell me more," she coaxed.

"I've started as a business consultant. Basically, a troubleshooter for businesses that are stagnant and want to grow and move forward, or that are experiencing difficulties but don't know where to start to fix them. I've always been the kind of person who needs to make everything right for other people and this gives me the opportunity to do that. Take Nickerson House for example."

She felt everything inside her protest. He wasn't about to tell her what to do with her business, was he? He gave a small chuckle.

"I can see by the look on your face you think I'm going to try to compel you to do something you don't want to, but I'm not, Stevie. Trust me. Nothing could be further from the truth. I don't have to go any further."

But her curiosity was piqued. "What were you going to tell me?"

"You know how much I want to see you succeed—on your own terms," he hastened to add. "So I got to thinking about your wellness spa and retreat and how you could make it work without doing the expansion you were initially planning for."

"You have a miracle solution for me?" she said skeptically.

"Not a miracle, exactly, more of a collaboration."

She narrowed her eyes. "With whom? You?"

"Oh, hell, no." He laughed again. "With a couple of the day spas in town. You could still provide the full exclusive retreat immersion experience with your existing accommodation and meals and hikes, but contract out the day spa experiences to local businesses. It would be a mutually satisfying experience for everyone involved, from clients through to the business owners.

"I know it's not what you wanted to do, but it would certainly set you on the path to get there. Worked in around the gourmet cooking weekends, I could imagine that you'd be operating at full, or near full, capacity on a regular basis all year around."

"And this is what you do now? Find solutions for people?"

He looked a little taken aback. "You don't like the idea?"

She turned it over in her mind. "No, I don't like it, I actually love it. I can't believe I didn't think of it myself. Thank you."

"You're welcome. I just want you to have the best of everything. Unconditionally."

Stevie felt a warm wave of emotion wash over her at his words. She believed him, every single thing he'd said. And she could see by the light burning in his eyes that he was passionate about his new business. As passionate as he'd been about her? The thought snuck up and tweaked inside her mind. Not wanting to examine her own feelings any deeper on that score, she asked him more questions.

"So you're obviously still based in Norfolk?"

"Yes, and you'd be proud of me. I've bought furniture for the house, too," he said with a wry smile.

He took another sip of his wine and she found her eyes glued to his mouth, to the moisture glistening on his lips. Unthinking, she moistened her own with the tip of her tongue, as if by doing so she could taste his, but it wasn't the same. She pushed the thought away. This was why she'd told herself she couldn't be with him. It made her want him too much and she didn't know how to handle that. It made her uncomfortable, needy in ways she'd sworn she'd never succumb to again. To distract herself this time, she rose from the table and cleared their plates before getting their dessert from the oven.

"You made blueberry pie?" he asked in clear admiration.

"With homemade ice cream, too, although I can't take credit for the ice cream," she said with a smile as she set the pie on the table and put bowls out before getting the ice cream from the freezer. She handed him a knife. "Here, you do the honors."

He cut generous slabs of pie for each of them and she added scoops of ice cream, which immediately began to melt and drizzle over the piecrust.

"This looks almost too good to eat," he said in admiration.

She shrugged. "Personally, I think it's too good to waste."

"Believe me, I'm not planning to waste a single bit of it."

As they ate, Stevie pondered the question that most plagued her. The only way she'd know was if she straight-out asked him.

"So, this new career path—it really sounds like you've found your niche, but specifically why now?" she blurted.

Fletcher swallowed what was in his mouth and looked at her. "You know, all my life, I've been trying to fit into someone else's mold. Son, brother, fiancé, friend, CEO. But I never felt like I was being honest about who *I* want to be. I was just going through the motions. Doing what was expected of me. And I've done that for so long I've kind of lost track of what my dreams and aspirations were.

"You had a lot to do with my decision to make a change. The pregnancy aside, you had the courage to start again. To make your life your own. I deeply admire that about you, and I understand your determination to protect your sense of self and not lose it pleasing someone else. I'd also like the chance for us to see how we can be better friends so we can be better parents."

He made it sound so simple, and the way he'd phrased it didn't leave her feeling uncomfortable. In fact, when he got up and began to help with clearing the kitchen and restoring it to its usual pristine state, it felt companionable. And when he left, with nothing more than a kiss on her cheek before heading to his car, she found herself feeling lonely. As if something vital had left the building—something vital to her.

Stevie made her way upstairs to her room and curled up on the chaise longue she had beside the bay window of her bedroom. She stared outside into the approaching darkness of the night and forced herself to examine her feelings for Fletcher. He was not the man she'd always thought he was, and that was probably why she was so drawn to him. Deep down, they were both lost souls and they were lucky to have found one another. He wasn't trying to manipulate or change her. He just wanted to be with her. The her *she* wanted to be.

She rolled that truth over in her mind and realized, too, that thinking about never seeing Fletcher again was far more painful to her than she wanted to admit. Another truth bloomed from deep in her chest. She was in love with him. Despite everything she'd done to stop it happening and to push him away, her heart had recognized him for the man he truly was. A man she could spend her future with. A man who was the father of her baby. She remembered the action that had started it all. The choice she'd made to go to his room. To take something for herself. And what she'd gained with it.

Without thinking a moment longer, Stevie grabbed her phone and pressed his number.

"Stevie, is everything okay?" he asked as he picked up on the first ring.

"Could you come back?"

"What time tomorrow were you thinking?"

"Not tomorrow," she said then paused to draw in a deep breath. "Now."

"Hold on, I'll be there in a few minutes."

He severed the call, not even asking why she wanted him. It was enough for him to know she needed him. That, more than anything spoke volumes about the kind of support he offered her. *Unconditionally*, as he'd said at dinner. Did that mean he loved her, too? When she heard his car pull into the driveway, she ran down the main stairs and flew out the front door and to the parking lot. Before he could speak, she reached up and put her hands on either side of his face and pulled him down to kiss him.

She poured everything she was into that kiss. Everything that made her the complicated and mixed-up, stubborn woman she was. But a woman who loved him nonetheless. When she could, she broke free, both of them breathing heavily.

"Come back inside," she said and began tugging him behind her as she made for the stairs that led to the front door.

"Stevie, what's going on?"

Once inside, she kissed him again. As she drew away a second time, she took both his hands in hers and looked into his face.

"Do you love me?"

His eyes grew dark and intense and she saw a

glimpse of caution there, as if he was afraid to reveal his true feelings in case she threw them back in his face. But then his expression cleared.

"With all my heart."

"I want you to stay," she said simply.

Confusion clouded his expression. "Tonight? I thought you still needed time and space."

"No, not tonight. Forever. I don't want time and space. I want you to become part of my personal space, so I'm never alone again. I need you and I love you. Please, won't you stay?"

He groaned and drew her into his arms. "Stevie, you have no idea how much that means to me. I promise you I will spend every day of my life making sure you don't regret your decision."

"I don't do regret," she said. "Not anymore."

Stevie pushed the front door closed behind them, shutting out their old lives so that they could enter their new one, safe in the knowledge that their love would be strong enough to build a future together they could both be proud of.

* * * * *

#2863 WHAT HAPPENS ON VACATION...

Westmoreland Legacy: The Outlaws • by Brenda Jackson

Alaskan senator Jessup Outlaw needs an escape...and he finds just the right one on his Napa Valley vacation: actress Paige Novak. What starts as a fling soon gets serious, but a familiar face from Paige's past may ruin everything...

#2864 THE RANCHER'S RECKONING

Texas Cattleman's Club: Fathers and Sons • by Joanne Rock

Pursuing the story of a lifetime, reporter Sierra Morgan reunites a lost baby with his father, rancher Colt Black. He's claiming his heir but needs Sierra's help as a live-in nanny. Will this temporary arrangement withstand the sparks and secrets between them?

#2865 WRONG BROTHER, RIGHT KISS

Dynasties: DNA Dilemma • by Joss Wood

As his brother's ex-wife, Tinsley Ryder-White is off-limits to Cody Gallant. Until one unexpected night of passion after a New Year's kiss leaves them reeling...and keeping their distance until forced to work together. Can they ignore the attraction that threatens their careers and hearts?

#2866 THE ONE FROM THE WEDDING

Destination Wedding • by Katherine Garbera

Jewelry designer Danni Eldridge didn't expect to see Leo Bisset at this destination-wedding weekend. The CEO once undermined her work; now she'll take him down a peg. But one hot night changes everything—until they realize they're competing for the same lucrative business contract.

#2867 PLAYING BY THE MARRIAGE RULES

by Fiona Brand

To secure his inheritance, oil heir Damon Wyatt needs to marry by midnight. But when his convenient bride never arrives, he's forced to cut a marriage deal with wedding planner Jenna Beaumont, his ex. Will this fake marriage resurrect real attraction?

#2868 OUT OF THE FRIEND ZONE

LA Women • by Sheri WhiteFeather

Reconnecting at a high school reunion, screenwriter Bailey Mitchell and tech giant Wade Butler can't believe how far they've come and how much they've missed one another. Soon they begin a passionate romance, one that might be derailed by a long-held secret...

HDCNM0222

SPECIAL EXCERPT FROM

⬦ HARLEQUIN

DESIRE

*After the loss of his brother, rancher Nick Hartmann is
suddenly the guardian of his niece. Enter Rose Kelly—
the new tutor. Sparks fly, but with his ranch at stake and
the secrets she's keeping, there's a lot at risk for both...*

Read on for a sneak peek at
Montana Legacy
by Katie Frey.

The ranch was more than a birthright—it was the thing that
made him a Hartmann. His dad made him promise. Maybe
Nick couldn't voice why that promise was important to him.
Why he cared. His brothers shrugged the responsibility so
easily, but he was shackled by it. His legacy couldn't be
losing the thing that had made him. No. He couldn't fail at
this. Not even to be with her, the mermaid incarnate.

She smiled her odd half smile and splashed some water
at him again. "I don't think you even know all you want,
cowboy." She bit her lip, drawing his attention instantly to
the one thing he'd wanted since meeting her at the airport.
He followed her in a second lap of the pool, catching up to
her in the deep end.

"So your brother married your prom date?" She widened
her eyes as she issued her question.

"It was a long time ago." He cleared his throat. Maybe
Ben was right and he needed to open up a bit.

"Yes, you're practically ancient, aren't you?" She swatted
a bit of water in his direction, which he managed to sidestep.

"Careful, Oxford." He smiled, unable to help himself. It felt good to smile, even more so when faced with the crushing sadness he'd been shouldering for the past three weeks.

"Can you not call me that?" She paused. "My sister went to Oxford. And I don't want to think about her right now."

Her bottom lip jutted forward and quivered. It provoked a response he was unprepared for, and he sealed her concern with a kiss so thorough it rocked him.

Everything he wanted to say he said with the kiss. *I'm sorry. I want you. I'm hurting. Let's forget this.* Her body, hot against his, was a welcome heat to balance the chill of the pool. It was soft and deliciously curved. The perfect answer to his desperate question.

His tongue parried hers and she opened to him with an earnestness that rocked him. A soft mew of submission and he lifted her legs around his, arousal pressed plainly against her. She wrapped her legs around him, the thin skin of the bathing suit a poor barrier, and bit gently at his lip.

"I'm sorry," he started.

"Let's not be sorry, not now." Gone was the sorrow. Instead, she looked at him with a burning fire that he matched with his own.

Don't miss what happens next in
Montana Legacy
by Katie Frey.

Available April 2022 wherever
Harlequin Desire books and ebooks are sold.

Harlequin.com

Love Harlequin romance?

DISCOVER.
Be the first to find out about promotions, news and exclusive content!

Facebook.com/HarlequinBooks

Twitter.com/HarlequinBooks

Instagram.com/HarlequinBooks

Pinterest.com/HarlequinBooks

YouTube.com/HarlequinBooks

ReaderService.com

EXPLORE.
Sign up for the Harlequin e-newsletter and download a free book from any series at **TryHarlequin.com**

CONNECT.
Join our Harlequin community to share your thoughts and connect with other romance readers!
Facebook.com/groups/HarlequinConnection

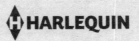

HARLEQUIN

Heartfelt or thrilling, passionate or uplifting—Harlequin is more than just happily-ever-after.

With twelve different series to choose from and new books available every month, you are sure to find stories that will move you, uplift you, inspire and delight you.